BOUNTY HUNTER NATE LANDRY: DANGEROUS DISGUISES

Mark L. Redmond

Contents

Chapter 1

———•◦❊◦•———

"Are you tired of my company?" Katie Whitman asked. She sat across the table from me, holding her coffee cup in both hands.

I noticed a hint of a smile on her lips as I nearly choked on a mouthful of biscuit. I had to wash the biscuit down with a swallow of coffee before I could reply. We were the only people left at the table, but I glanced around to be sure the dining room was empty.

"What?" I asked. "No, Ma'am—Katie—why would you ask me that?"

I had been a guest at Mrs. Whitman's boarding house for almost two weeks on my second stay. A few months earlier, Wolf had brought me to her place after I'd been shot, and I had stayed until the doctor thought I was fit to ride a horse. This time I had come to spend some time with Katie.

"You haven't spoken for a quarter of an hour," she said. Katie was smiling now, but I saw concern in her eyes.

"I was eating my delicious breakfast," I said. "I don't reckon I could ever get tired of your company."

"But you're leaving soon," she said. "I wish you'd stay."

Four years ago, when I'd lost my wife Elizabeth and our newborn baby at the same time, I had locked the door to my heart. I hadn't found a reason to open it again.

1

Then Katie came along. I couldn't explain how she did it, but she opened that door, walked into my heart, and made herself at home.

"I wish I could stay," I said, "but I have work to do." I had been looking at my plate. When I looked at Katie, she was still smiling; but her beautiful brown eyes were brimming with tears. She blinked them away, stood, and began to clear the table.

Picking up my plate, fork, and cup, I followed her to the kitchen. "What can I do to help?" I asked.

She filled two cups with coffee and set them on a silver tray, along with a plate of biscuits, some butter, and a small cup of honey. "A man and his wife arrived late last night," she said. "They asked if they could sleep through breakfast but still have coffee and biscuits." She added two napkins, a knife, two spoons, and two forks to the tray. "Would you please take this tray to the last room on the left? I reckon they're awake by now."

"Yes, Ma'am," I said.

I'm not often surprised because I plan carefully and think through the situations I face when I'm tracking someone. Delivering a breakfast tray was a simple task that required neither thinking nor planning. I carried the tray to the end of the hallway and tapped on the door. When a woman opened it, I almost dropped the tray. I was looking into the eyes of Leah Fulton.

The look on her face told me she was just as surprised as I was. Before I could speak, Leah grabbed the tray and kicked the door shut; and as I reached for the knob, I heard the lock click.

When I entered the kitchen, Katie was washing the breakfast dishes. She spoke without turning around.

"Thank you for delivering breakfast to the Carsons," she said. "I don't usually serve breakfast to folks in their rooms; but they seemed like nice people, and they were so tired that I thought—" she had picked up a towel and was wiping a plate as she turned toward me. Her smile disappeared. "Nate," she said, "what's wrong?"

I picked up my hat and started toward the door. "I'll explain when I get back," I said. "I need to talk to the marshal."

When I walked into the house ten minutes later, Katie had finished washing the dishes and was wiping the table. She stopped, hung the cloth over the back of a chair, and motioned toward the parlor with one hand.

"Can we sit while you tell me what's happened?" she asked.

She led me to a settee and sat beside me, turned so she was facing me. "You look as if you've seen a ghost," she said.

"Not a ghost," I said. I turned to face her. "A dust devil."

Katie listened without interrupting as I told her about Tom and Leah Fulton. When I had finished, she whispered, "Why is she here?"

"I don't know," I said, "but I reckon I'm going to find out."

"Shouldn't we wait until Marshal Becker gets here?" she asked.

"He's not coming," I replied. "He wasn't in his office."

When I stood, Katie grabbed my arm with both hands. "What are you doing?" she asked.

3

I lifted my arm slightly and stepped back, pulling Katie to her feet. "I'm going back to her room," I said. "I'm going to take Leah Fulton—and most likely the man who's with her—to the jail. If the marshal isn't back yet, I'll lock them up myself."

Katie was still holding onto my arm. "Aren't they dangerous?" she asked.

I covered her hands with one of mine. "She is," I said, "and I reckon he is too if he's travelling with her. That's why I want to get her out of your house."

She let go of my arm and looked up at me. "I want to help," she said. "Let me get my gun."

Katie walked out of the parlor; and when she returned, she was carrying a new Colt revolver. She looked nervous but determined.

"What I need you to do," I said, "is stay here, pray, and keep your gun ready."

"I can do that," she said. "Please be careful."

"I will," I said. I smiled at her. "I don't want to break something and have you add its cost to my bill."

When I knocked on the door to Leah's room, I stood to one side. Sometimes when people don't want to have company, they fire a weapon through the door instead of opening it. Since I've never enjoyed being shot, I try to stay out of the way.

Nobody shot through the door. Nobody opened it either. I knocked again, but I still got no response. I turned the knob and pushed, but the door was still locked. Because I didn't want to have the cost of a broken door added to my bill, I turned and walked toward the parlor.

"Don't shoot, Katie," I said. "It's only me."

She stood just outside the parlor, holding her gun in both hands with it pointed at the floor. Her hands trembled a little, but she still had a determined look on her face. She let out her breath as if she'd been holding it for a long time.

"I need a key," I said. Without speaking, Katie hurried away. When she returned a minute later, she dropped a key into my outstretched hand and stepped back, still holding her revolver.

At the door, I slid the key into the lock and turned it as quietly as I could, again standing to one side. After turning the knob, I pushed on the door. As it swung open without making a sound, I whispered my thanks to Katie for keeping the hinges greased.

Holding my six-gun at arm's length to cover the room, I stepped inside. What I found—or, I should say, what I didn't find—was no surprise. The room was empty. A pale blue curtain danced in the breeze that came through the open window. Fresh scuff marks on the sill told me how Leah and her friend had left the room.

Lowering the hammer on my gun, I holstered it and ran toward the parlor, calling to Katie from the hall. She was still standing outside the parlor where I had left her.

"They went out the window!" I said. "I'm going to try to keep them from leaving town."

"What can I do to help?" Katie asked.

Halfway out the door, I stopped and looked at her. "See if the marshal is back in his office," I said. "If he is, tell him what's happened and ask him to help me find them." I turned to go.

"Wait!" Katie said. "What if he's not back yet?"

"Come back here and wait for me," I said. "I'll be back."

As I pulled the door closed behind me, I heard her say, "You'd better come back, Nate Landry."

Since Katie's house had been built at the edge of town, only open country lay to my left. To my right, the street ran all the way to the opposite side of town. Both sides of the street were lined with businesses, and both sides were full of people. Leah and the man with her would be among the people who were walking away from me.

Most of the folks that lined the street didn't appear to be in a hurry. I turned down the first alley I came to. When I reached the path that ran along the backs of the buildings, parallel to the main street, I broke into a run. The livery stable stood at the far end of town, and I needed to reach it before Leah and her companion did.

The morning was cool but damp, and the dark clouds held a promise of more rain. By the time I stopped at the back of the livery to catch my breath, I was sweating. As I walked along the side of the building, I searched for anything that looked, sounded, or even smelled wrong.

When I reached the street, I leaned against the side of the livery and watched for Leah, but I saw no sign of her or her friend. Still watching, I crossed to the open double doors in the center of the front wall.

A few feet inside the doorway, an old man who resembled a scarecrow sat hunched forward on a wooden keg, smoking a pipe. When he saw me, he smiled, removed the pipe from his mouth, and pointed at me with its stem.

"Good morning, young feller," he said. "What can I do fer you?"

"Good morning," I said. "I was hoping to meet some folks here, but I don't see them." I smiled. "I don't know if I've showed up too early or too late."

The old man tapped his pipe against the side of the keg to knock out the ashes. "How many people, and what do these folks look like?" he asked. He pulled a worn leather pouch from one of his vest pockets, loosened the drawstring that held it closed, and began to refill the pipe with fresh tobacco.

"A man and a woman," I said. I described Leah. "I've never seen the man before," I said, "and they would have been here within the last half hour."

He returned the pouch to his pocket, pulled a lucifer from another pocket, and lit his pipe. Shaking his head slowly, he exhaled a small cloud of smoke. "From the way you described this lady," he said, "I reckon I'd remember seeing her; but she hasn't come through here."

I thanked him and had started to leave when a thought struck me and turned me around. "Who works here at night?" I asked.

"The feller who owns this place," he said, "Bob Stratton."

"Where can I find Bob?" I asked.

He grinned. "You're talking to him. My night man quit a couple weeks back, and I ain't found a replacement fer him yet." Still grinning, he asked, "You lookin' fer work?"

I grinned back at him. "Not today," I said. "These folks rode in late last night. Did they leave their horses here?"

He shook his head. "Last night was quiet," he said. "Nobody came by after ten o'clock."

As I walked down the street toward Katie's place, I thought about seeing Leah. I had seen surprise in her face, but not fear. I reckoned she would have wanted to get out of Phoenix as quickly as possible after discovering I was in town.

When I had returned to her room, it was empty except for the breakfast tray. I hadn't paid attention at the time, but the coffee cups were still half full, and only one or two biscuits were missing. Leah and her friend had left through the window before I had finished telling Katie about them.

Using the same alley I had followed on the way to the livery, I arrived at the back of Katie's house. What I found confirmed my suspicions. After learning the location of their room, Leah and her companion had hobbled their horses near their room to provide a quick escape if they needed it.

By going to the livery, I would have caught most outlaws before they could leave town. I had forgotten that I was dealing with the Dust Devil.

Chapter 2

-------•⊱✳⊰•-------

"Where do you reckon they're headed?" Katie asked. We sat in rocking chairs on her front porch, drinking coffee.

"Mrs. Whitman," I said, "I believe you must have me confused with someone who has a clue." I drank some of my coffee. "The main thing Wolf and I learned from tracking Leah Fulton is that whatever you think she'll do next is most likely not going to happen." I turned to look at Katie. "I would have bet a twenty-dollar gold piece that she was at least a hundred miles from the Arizona Territory by now, but she shows up in Phoenix."

"Maybe she's looking for you," Katie said. I smiled, but Katie didn't.

"Why would she be looking for me?" I asked. She took a sip of her coffee and then looked at me.

"I reckon," she said, "Leah blames you for Tom's death."

"I didn't kill Tom," I said.

Katie raised her eyebrows. "You and I know you didn't kill Tom," she said, "but does Leah know? She could be looking for revenge."

"I hadn't thought about that possibility," I said, "but you may be right."

We drank our coffee and watched the townsfolk on the street. After a few minutes, Katie spoke.

"Maybe God put Leah at my place so you'd know she's coming for you."

"Maybe He did," I said.

"Are you going after her?" she asked.

"I can't," I said.

Leaning back in her chair, she gave me a puzzled look. "Why not?" she asked.

"Because," I replied, "I promised a very special lady I'd be here for two weeks, and I still have three days left before I'll have fulfilled that promise."

We watched the folks on the street in silence for a few minutes. When Katie turned toward me, her eyes brimmed with tears. "Do I really mean that much to you?" she asked.

As I reached my hand toward her and she took it, her first tear fell. "Yes, Ma'am," I said, "you do."

For the next hour, Katie and I sat on her porch, talking, drinking coffee, and enjoying each other's company. After a few minutes of silence, Katie let out a long sigh.

"As much as I'd like to spend the day sitting here with you," she said, "I don't reckon my work will get done unless I get out of this chair and do it." She stood and held out her hand to take my cup.

I handed it to her and stood, facing her. "Is there anything I can do to help you?" I asked.

Katie smiled. "Do bounty hunters wash bedding, clean rooms, and prepare food for boarders?" she asked.

"I reckon they might," I said, "if they were properly motivated."

Katie laughed. "Thank you, but I have a woman who helps me for a few hours each day. Martha should be here soon. Do you reckon you can find something to do for a while?"

"Yes, Ma'am, I do," I said. I touched my hat brim and opened the door for her. "I'll be back sometime this afternoon," I said. I closed the door behind her, stepped off the porch, and headed down the street toward the marshal's office.

This time, I found Marshal Becker in his office. Although I had seen him a few times during my stay at Katie's boarding house, I had never spoken to him. He was seated at his desk when I walked into the room. He stood, walked to meet me and shook my hand as I introduced myself.

"John Becker," he said. "What can I do for you, Mr. Landry?"

"Nate," I said.

After I told him what I wanted, he waved me to a chair. Picking up a tin cup from the desk, he walked to a stove in the corner, used a piece of leather to pick up a battered pot, and filled the cup with steaming coffee. He looked at me over his shoulder.

"It's fresh Arbuckles', and I have another cup," he said.

I'd be obliged," I said.

We sat on opposite sides of his desk, drinking coffee while he looked through his wanted posters. When he laid the last one aside, he looked at me.

"Nate," he said, "I'm not saying there's no bounty on this woman." He drank some coffee, set his cup on the desk, and stroked his chin. "I'm just saying I don't have a poster yet. I wish I could be

11

more help to you. I'll let you know if I learn anything about her while you're still in town."

I thanked John and left his office. Crossing the street, I walked toward the livery. Mac was probably getting tired of being cooped up in a corral, and I wanted to do some thinking, so I reckoned a ride would do us both some good.

The old livery man was dozing in a chair that leaned against the wall of the first stall. Not seeing a need to wake him, I took Mac's bridle from a wooden peg on the wall, left the livery, and walked to the gate of the corral. Mac was waiting for me.

When I rode out of town a few minutes later, the old man was still asleep. I held Mac to a walk until we had cleared the edge of town, and then I let him run. When he finally slowed to a canter, we were still surrounded by flat, brush-covered country. I reined Mac to a walk and looked around for some shade, but the closest outcropping of rock was more than half a mile away.

"Well, Pardner," I said, "I hadn't planned on going that far away from town, but I reckon that outcropping is the closest spot around to get some thinking done." I patted Mac's neck. "If you'll get us over there, I'll make it up to you with extra grain when we get back to town."

Always motivated by the offer of extra food, Mac headed for the outcropping at a canter. The breeze was light, and the morning was still cool enough for most of the desert critters to be active. As I watched the brush around me, I saw quail, jackrabbits, horned toads, a roadrunner with a snake hanging from its beak, coyotes, and several rattlesnakes. From farther away, three mule deer watched us;

and overhead five or six buzzards circled slowly in their never-ending search for food.

We had approached the outcropping from the shady side. Although the day hadn't become hot yet, the coolness of the shade felt good. I stepped down from the saddle and looped the reins around the horn. Most of the sparse grass I could see grew close to the outcropping, so I reckoned Mac wouldn't stray too far.

After checking for rattlers, I unrolled my bedroll, folded it in half, and laid it on a flat rock. Guessing I'd have about an hour before I lost my shade, I sat on my blanket and leaned against the boulder behind me.

I've never been a man who lives in the past. Wolf and I had seen horrible things happen during the war, but after the war had ended, we left it behind us. When we encountered other men who'd fought in the war, we never asked them about which side they'd chosen. It didn't matter to us. We had seen bad things happen since the war too, but we had left those things in the past as well.

The memory I couldn't escape was one that always crept into my mind during quiet times. It also haunted my dreams.

When Wolf and I returned to the Arizona Territory at the end of the war, Elizabeth had been waiting for me. Six months later, our wedding marked the beginning of the happiest two years of my life. She had been my best friend.

A year later when Elizabeth told me we were going to have a child, I was overwhelmed by God's goodness. When the day came for the baby to be born, Wolf and I waited outside the cabin while the doctor helped Elizabeth with the delivery. When the doctor came out of the cabin, he told me I had lost both my wife and my child.

Something inside me had died that day too. I didn't blame God for taking away a gift that He had given me; I just didn't understand. That part of me that had been filled with love for Elizabeth had been closed off for the past four years, and I reckoned it would remain closed for the rest of my life.

I smiled as I recalled again how God had unlocked the door and let Katie in. When she walked into that closed-up part of me, she filled it with sunshine.

After a while, I realized I had been sitting on that flat rock, grinning and thinking about Katie when I should have been trying to figure out how I was going to catch Leah and send her to prison.

The shade was gone, and the rock where I sat had begun to heat up. I stood, shook out my bedroll, rolled it up, and fastened it behind my saddle. After taking a drink from my canteen, I poured water into my hat and let Mac drink. Just as I started to saddle up, a bullet hit the rocks above me and whined away.

Grabbing my rifle from its scabbard, I ducked behind the closest rock. When no more shots followed the first one, I raised my head a few inches to see if I could see the shooter. At first, I saw no one, but then a movement caught my eye. What I saw didn't make sense. Two riders were facing me from a distance beyond the range of my Winchester. One of them waved an arm over his head. Then both riders turned and rode away from town.

I watched until they were out of sight. I walked to Mac and climbed into the saddle, but I rode with my rifle across my lap. I leaned forward and patted Mac's neck.

"If you have an explanation for what just happened, Pardner," I said, "I'm listening." When he didn't reply, we continued toward town in silence.

The bullet had struck the rock at least ten feet above me and about the same distance to the shooter's left. He was either a bad shot, or he was only giving me a warning. In either case, the man had to be using a Sharps rifle to hit so close to me from that distance.

The waving seemed like a mocking gesture, and I couldn't make any sense of that either. Although I held Mac to a walk all the way back to town to give me time to think, I was still puzzled when I stepped down from the saddle in front of the livery.

I took care of Mac before I turned him loose in the corral. I hung his bridle on the peg where I'd found it and turned to leave the livery.

"Your friends finally showed up a little while after you left," the old timer said. I turned in time to see him walking toward me from the back of the stable, carrying a pitchfork in one hand.

"What friends?" I asked.

He leaned the pitchfork against the wall, sat in his chair, and removed his battered hat. "I reckon they were the ones you was asking about—a man and a lady." He pulled a bandana from his pocket and wiped the sweat from his face. "I told 'em which way you rode out, and they headed that way too. Did they catch up with you?"

"I didn't get to talk to them," I said.

"Well, in that case," he said, "I have a message for you from the lady." He picked up a canteen that lay on the floor beside his chair, pulled out the cork, and took a long drink. He replaced the cork and dropped the canteen on the floor. "She said to tell you she was sorry she missed you, but she wouldn't miss you the next time. She was looking forward to surprising you with a gift like the one you gave Tom."

I thanked the old timer and started to leave the livery. Stopping, I looked over my shoulder. "You were asleep when I left," I said. "How did you know which way I rode?"

"Sometimes a feller closes his eyes so he can sleep," the old timer said, "and sometimes he closes them so no one will pester him." He was grinning when I left the livery.

As I walked toward Katie's place, I understood what Leah's intentions were. I earned a living as a hunter, but Leah Fulton and her friend planned to turn me into the hunted. Somehow, I needed to keep that from happening.

Chapter 3

---•➤✦←•---

When I got to Katie's house, I didn't go inside. Instead, I sat in the chair I'd used earlier. I didn't want to disturb Katie while she was working, and I needed some time to think.

If Leah Fulton blamed me for Tom's death, I reckoned she blamed Wolf too. The easiest way to kill both of us was to wait until we were together. Since we didn't know when we'd be together again or where we'd meet, she'd have to follow one of us.

I wouldn't underestimate Leah. She had plenty of money, and she was a clever woman. She had found me by chance, but she couldn't know where Wolf was. I didn't know where he was.

I had been leaning back in my chair, but something occurred to me that made me sit up straight. The odds that Leah would be in Phoenix, especially at the same time I was, were long. Her being at Katie's house at the same time I was couldn't be a coincidence. Leah must have known I was there. She had been surprised when I knocked at the door of her room, but my bringing her breakfast had to have let Leah know I was there to see Katie. Now Katie could be in danger too.

The door opened, and I stood as Katie and another woman stepped onto the porch. Both ladies wore aprons, and both had rolled up their sleeves. Katie smiled when she saw me.

"This is my friend and helper, Martha Sands," she said. I removed my hat and smiled.

"Martha, this is my friend, Nate Landry," Katie said. Martha smiled.

"I'm pleased to meet you, Ma'am," I said.

As Martha walked away, I said, "She looks enough like you to be your sister."

Katie brushed a loose strand of hair off her forehead. "That's what folks keep telling us," she said. "My heart thinks she's my sister." She looked up at me. "How long have you been sitting out here? You should have come in!"

"It's a beautiful day," I said, "and I didn't want to get in your way."

Still looking up at me, she smiled. "I'm working on supper," she said. "I have three other people besides us to feed tonight. You can either help or just keep me company while I'm cooking."

Since I've never been much good at sitting around while other folks work, I rolled up my sleeves and washed my hands. Katie nodded toward a stack of dishes on the sideboard.

"Would you mind setting the table?" she asked. I picked up the dishes and carried them to the table.

"Whatever you're cooking," I said, "sure smells good."

"I'm making a beef stew," she said. Katie stopped working and looked over her shoulder. "I hope you like it."

The table could seat twelve people. I put a plate in front of the first two chairs on each side of the table and the chair at the end. "Beef stew is one of my favorites," I said, "especially if you're cooking it. Will this work?"

"Perfectly," she said. "Sharing the food is much easier when people are seated together." She lifted a board, covered with the meat she had been cutting up, stepped over to the stove, and used her knife to scrape the meat into a large pot of boiling broth. "Those bowls are for the stew, and the plates are for sourdough bread or corn bread."

"Or both?" I asked.

Katie smiled. "Or both," she said. She washed the cutting board and scrubbed several large yucca roots. As she began to slice the yucca, she asked, "What did you do today?"

I had already decided to tell Katie about Leah if she asked, but I'd been hoping she wouldn't ask until later. As I laid a fork, a knife, and a spoon beside each plate, I thought of ways to put off telling her until after supper.

"Mac and I went out of town to give him some exercise and give me a chance to do some thinking."

She didn't turn around, but her shoulders stiffened. I could tell she had paused in her slicing. "Oh," she said. "What were you thinking about?"

I placed a coffee cup next to each plate. "Mostly you, I reckon," I said.

"Good thoughts?" she asked. She began to slice the yucca again. She hadn't looked at me.

"Mostly good," I said. I was grinning, but when Katie laid the knife beside the cutting board and turned to face me, her lower lip trembled slightly, and her eyes brimmed with tears.

"*Mostly* good?" she asked.

"No, Katie," I said. "*All* good. My thoughts about you are always good."

When she turned around and began to slice the yucca root again, I let out a long breath and whispered a prayer of thanks that I had been able to correct my not-so-funny blunder. Then I heard Katie's first sob.

"Katie," I said, "please forgive me." Stepping behind her, I placed my hands on her shoulders. "I didn't mean to hurt your feelings."

When she turned toward me and pressed her face against my chest, she was sobbing uncontrollably. I stood there, feeling stupid, wondering what to do. As Katie continued to cry, I wrapped my arms around her and held her gently. I said nothing because I had no idea what the right thing to say was.

After what seemed like half an hour but was probably only five minutes, Katie stopped crying. I was already a bit confused about what had just happened, but she really muddied the water.

Leaning back, she looked into my eyes, shook her head slightly, and smiled. "Oh, Nate," she said, "how could you think I was upset by what you said?"

"I reckon," I said, "it might be because you started crying right after I said it." I still had my arms around Katie. She put her arms around me, hugged me, laid her head against my chest, and sighed.

"You need to forgive me," she whispered.

The muddied water turned to quicksand, and I was in it up to my neck. I held her without speaking, hoping she'd say something to at least give me a hint about what was happening. I was thankful she couldn't see the confused look on my face.

"I'm just being selfish," she said.

I felt the quicksand touch my chin. In desperation, I asked, "What do you mean, Katie?"

When she leaned back and looked up at me, her cheeks were wet again. "I don't want you to leave so soon," she said.

Experience had taught me that thinking about what you're going to say before you say it is usually the best practice. I don't reckon I was thinking much about anything but Katie right then because I just said, "That makes two of us. I love you, Katie Whitman."

I can't begin to explain what happened next. Katie's beautiful brown eyes widened. "I love you too, Nate Landry!" she said. Then she slid her hands up to the back of my neck, pulled my head down, kissed me, and started crying again.

I reckon some folks might think two people couldn't fall in love during a two-week visit, and don't know for certain I'd disagree with them. I couldn't speak for Katie right then; but for my part, something had started to stir my heart while Katie was nursing me back to health after I'd been shot in the head a few months back. I just couldn't imagine at the time why a woman like her would ever have any interest in a man like me. It still didn't make any sense.

During the rest of the time we spent preparing supper, Katie and I didn't talk much; but we did kiss again—twice—and I hugged her and told her again that I loved her. I reckon it was the fact that both of us wanted to talk in private that made supper seem to drag on forever. When it was finally over, all three guests wandered away, headed for a saloon, their room, or outside to sit on the porch.

I helped Katie clear the dishes from the table and stack them on the sideboard in the kitchen. Taking a few at a time from the stacks, she washed the dishes in a large tub she had placed in the dry sink. After washing each plate, bowl, or cup, she rinsed it in a smaller tub, handed it to me, and I dried it. We talked as we worked.

"I don't reckon I've ever been this happy," Katie said.

"I feel the same," I said. I finished drying a cup and set it on the sideboard. "But I don't know where we'll go from here."

"We do need to talk about that," she said. She washed a fork and dropped it into the rinse tub. "Let's have some coffee in the parlor when we're finished here."

Something like half an hour later, Katie and I sat beside each other in the parlor, drinking coffee and not talking. Finally, Katie spoke. "Shouldn't one of us start a conversation?" she asked.

"Yes, Ma'am," I said. I drank the last of my coffee and set the cup on a small table beside me. Turning to look at Katie, I smiled. "Go ahead."

She had been sitting close to me, but she leaned away and looked at me with raised eyebrows. "I reckon a conversation like this one should be started by the gentleman, not the lady," she said.

"I apologize," I said. I was still smiling. "I don't have much experience with conversations like this."

It was Katie's turn to smile. "I certainly hope you don't," she said. She leaned against me again.

I cleared my throat, took a deep breath, and let it out through my mouth. Looking at Katie and smiling, I said, "Thank you for a delicious meal tonight. The coffee was excellent too!"

Trying not to smile, she asked, "What are you doing?"

I gave her my best confused look. "I reckon I'm starting a conversation," I said.

It's amazing that a single word, if spoken in the right tone, can convey more meaning than many sentences do.

"Nate," Katie said.

"Yes, Ma'am," I said. "I love you."

She wrapped both of her arms around my left arm and squeezed it. "I love you too," she said.

I leaned over and kissed her. "That's the simple part of what's happening with us," I said. "Everything beyond that gets complicated."

Katie let go of my arm and stood. "Excuse me for interrupting," she said, "but this conversation will probably be a long one. Let me get us more coffee."

A few minutes later, I swallowed a mouthful of strong, hot coffee and set my cup on the table beside me. I looked at Katie.

"Let's lay out the facts first," I said. "I'm a bounty hunter. I'm good at what I do. I don't reckon I'd be a good bank teller, store clerk, rancher, or school master. Being a bounty hunter pays well—better than any of these other professions—but it takes me all over Arizona and involves some danger."

I drank more coffee and smiled at Katie. "You have a steady, profitable business here, and it pays well too because you're good at what you do. If we can't figure out a way to make our businesses run at the same time, we'll have to close one of them — that is, if we want to — if we decide to —"

"To marry?" Katie asked. She was smiling, but she had tears in her eyes. "Why, Mr. Landry, are you asking me to marry you?"

I moved from my seat and knelt in front of her, taking her small hand in both of mine. "I reckon I am if you'll have me, Mrs. Whitman," Katie was crying too hard to speak, but she nodded her head.

I stood, took both of her hands, pulled her to her feet, and wrapped my arms around her. After a minute or so, I leaned down to kiss her. We stood there until she stopped crying, and then sat again.

"Before I continue," I said, "I need to ask you a question."

Katie dabbed her eyes with a handkerchief. "What?" she asked.

"Was that a 'yes'?" I asked.

Chapter 4

------••❋••------

Katie listened as I shared my thoughts with her. Although I wanted to continue being a bounty hunter, I saw two drawbacks. Whether or not Katie operated her boarding house, I'd be away from her for long periods of time while I chased outlaws by myself or with Wolf. I didn't like the idea of our being apart during those times.

I liked the second drawback even less. The outlaws I pursued generally either wound up in prison for a long time or dead for even longer. Every so often though, one of those outlaws escaped from prison or served his sentence and was released. If those men came hunting Wolf and me, they weren't usually looking to thank us for changing their lives. Leah Fulton wasn't planning to thank us either.

Wolf and I usually knew when someone was hunting us, and we accepted the danger as part of the job. If I married Katie and the outlaws found out, she could become a target for those who wanted to punish me.

When I stopped talking and drank more coffee, Katie remained silent. She sipped her coffee, holding her cup in both hands. After setting the cup on the table beside her, she looked at me.

"Is anyone besides Leah Fulton after you right now?" she asked.

"Not that I know of," I said. "Why do you ask?"

"Because," she said, "you and Wolf might have trouble focusing on hunting outlaws if you have to worry about someone hunting you, looking for a chance to shoot you in the back." She drank the last of her coffee. "In your line of work, being distracted could get you killed. You'd be in even more danger when you're chasing someone by yourself." She stood, picked up her cup in one hand, and held out the other hand for mine. I gave it to her.

"When Leah makes her play," I said, "she'll want to be facing me so I'll know she's the one who's going to stop me."

"You mean *kill* you," Katie said.

"Yes," I said, "and I reckon she'll want to take her time and make me suffer."

Katie shuddered. "I'll be right back," she said. When she returned a few minutes later, she brought a tray that held our coffee cups and a plate of cookies. She set the tray on the table beside me. As soon as she had seated herself, I handed her one of the cups and set the plate between us.

"In my opinion," she said, "capturing Leah before she has a chance to—to come after you, seems like the best idea."

"I agree," I said. I picked up a cookie and tasted it. "But I see two difficulties in following that plan." I took another bite of the cookie. "Do I taste molasses?" I asked. I was smiling, but Katie wasn't.

"Yes," she said. "What are the difficulties?"

I drank some coffee. "First," I said, "last time Wolf and I chased Leah, he named her *Dust Devil* because she's very good at not being caught."

Katie moved the plate of cookies to my lap and scooted closer to me. "You told me you and Wolf are really good at what you do," she said. "How could she have escaped?"

"We're exceedingly good at what we do," I said. "Leah didn't actually escape; we stopped chasing her."

"Why?" Katie asked. She took a cookie from the plate.

"When we told the bank president Tom was dead," I said, "we returned Tom's share of the stolen money and explained Leah's role in the robbery. The bank owner was happy to get even part of his money back, and he refused to believe Leah had anything to do with the robbery." I took another bite of my cookie and drank more coffee. "He thanked us, paid us, and sent us on our way."

Katie finished chewing a bite of cookie before she spoke. "Since no reward was offered," she said, "you and Wolf had no reason to track her down."

"Not one," I said, "and that's the second difficulty. I'm a bounty hunter. When Wolf rides with me, so is he." I finished my cookie and picked up another. "These are delicious," I said.

"Thank you," Katie said. She smiled and raised her eyebrows. "You were saying?"

"Oh," I said, "We're bounty hunters. We hunt people when somebody pays us to hunt them. If there's no bounty on a person—like Leah—we don't usually pursue that person."

"Unless that person—like Leah—is trying to kill you and Wolf," Katie said. She looked up at me and squeezed my arm.

"I reckon we could pursue someone if the reward was saving our lives," I said.

Katie let go of my arm, leaned back, and looked at me. "You *reckon* you could?" she asked.

"Well," I said, "we usually only work for money, but we can make an exception this one time."

"I have something to say," Katie said, "but I want to make sure of a few things first." She finished her coffee, set her cup on the table beside her, and moved away from me. "I want to look into your eyes without straining my neck. If God allows, we want to get married. Am I right?"

"Yes, Ma'am," I said. Katie smiled.

"I'm not getting rich, but I'm making a living by running this boarding house." She took a deep breath and let it out slowly as if she was trying to build up the courage to continue. I gave her my most encouraging smile. "Would you consider making Phoenix your home instead of Florence? Then we could keep this business as well as your bounty hunting, and we could live a little more comfortably."

"I reckon we could," I said, "if you'd be willing to give up the luxury of living in my cabin." When she laughed, I laid my hand on hers. "Your laugh is my favorite music."

Katie raised one hand to cover her lips. "Please don't make me cry again," she said. "I want to finish what I have to say." She folded her hands in her lap and continued. "From what you've told me, you're concerned that someone seeking revenge on you might come after me if he—or she found out we were married."

"I am," I said.

"For my part," she said, "although I know God watches over us, I would worry about you every time you rode away—with or without

Wolf—to pursue an outlaw." Katie took another deep breath, closed her eyes, and let it out slowly. "I don't want to live that way."

I felt as if somebody had kicked me in the stomach. Katie stared at her hands and said nothing. I reckoned I should say something to change her mind, but I couldn't find the right words. When I finally spoke, my throat was dry; and my voice was hoarse.

"So, you're saying there's no way we could ever get married?" I asked.

Katie gasped as her head snapped up. She looked at me with wide eyes. "Are you mad?" She moved close to me, took my face in her hands, and kissed me. A minute later when she stopped the kiss, she kept her hands on my face and looked into my eyes. "Why would you ask me that question?"

I kissed her again and then shrugged my shoulders. "I have no idea why," I said. "I thought it was your idea."

When Katie covered her face with both hands, I reckoned I'd made her cry again. I was more than a little surprised when she looked at me and I saw she was laughing. She wrapped both of her arms around one of mine.

"What I meant was," she said, "I don't want to live with us worrying about each other every time we're apart." Katie was trying not to smile.

"We can't keep that from happening," I said.

"Oh," she said, "I reckon we can." Katie let go of my arm and scooted away from me again to make it easier for her to see my face.

"I have two suggestions," she said, "but you have to promise me something before I tell you what they are."

It was my turn to raise my eyebrows. "I promise," I said.

Katie sighed. "I haven't told you what I need you to promise yet," she said.

"It doesn't matter what it is," I said, "but please pardon my interrupting you."

"You have to promise to listen to me until I've given you both suggestions," she said, "and you have to accept one of them."

"My answer," I said, "is still 'yes.' I promise."

"Since you're concerned that our getting married could result in some outlaw deciding to come after me in order to get revenge on you," Katie said, "we could—at least for a while—keep our marriage a secret. I've had other guests who stayed here for weeks at a time. We'd have to pretend to be just friends when other people are around, and we'd still have to be apart whenever you're on someone's trail, but—"

She must have seen that I was about to speak. Holding a finger to her lips and then pointing at me, she waited until I gave her a nod. Then she continued.

"I haven't had a chance to work through all the details yet," she said, "but if you choose this suggestion, I'm sure we can figure out a way to make it work."

I put on my best poker face so Katie wouldn't know what I thought of her suggestion. Keeping our marriage a secret had to be one of the worst ideas I'd ever heard. I reckoned her second suggestion had to be the better of the two—that is, until she told me what it was.

"My second suggestion is, in my opinion, the better of the two," she said, "because if you choose to follow this suggestion, we'll never have to be separated; consequently, we'll never worry about each other's safety."

Forgetting my promise about not interrupting her, I spoke. "I don't want to hide the fact that I love you," I said, "or that God blessed me by allowing me to marry you. I choose your second suggestion. I'll work in the mercantile, the livery—I'll be John's deputy—I don't care how I earn a living as long as I'm sharing my life with you."

For a few minutes, Katie looked at me without speaking. "You really mean that, don't you?" she asked.

"I do," I said.

"Good," she said. Leaning back a little, she folded her hands in her lap again. "I wasn't finished. My second suggestion doesn't involve your getting a job in town. I want you to keep the job you have and take me with you."

Chapter 5

Before Wolf and I joined the army, we had spent the better part of a year wandering through the Arizona Territory. Being young and curious, we just wanted to take a look around. One beautiful spring day in the northern part of the territory, we had dismounted and walked into a canyon to explore while our horses rested.

Jumping from one boulder to the next, Wolf and I moved deeper into the canyon until we eventually lost sight of each other. When I reached a place where the nearest boulder was beyond my leaping ability, I jumped to the floor of the canyon and landed in quicksand.

Struggling to get out of the quicksand only caused me to sink faster. By the time Wolf found me, I was waist deep in the muck and as scared as I'd ever been. I'd never felt so helpless—until right then, sitting in Katie's parlor and trying to think of something to say. Unlike that day in the canyon, this time I didn't have Wolf to pull me out of the mess I had gotten myself into.

"You and Wolf took Anna Thomas on the trail with you," Katie said. She scooted close to me and hugged my right arm with both of hers again. "I can ride as well as most men, and I'm a good shot with a rifle or a revolver. I can cook for us while we're trailing outlaws too."

I wanted to say what was on my mind, but I found it as empty as old Mother Hubbard's cupboard. Consequently, I said nothing.

"I reckon if we stay together," Katie said, "people like Leah Fulton will have a harder time getting to us—whether Wolf is with us, or it's just you and me on a trail."

After we had sat in silence for what seemed like a long time, she spoke again. "Are you angry with me, Nate?" she asked.

Her question surprised me, and I chuckled. Katie relaxed her grip on my arm, folded her hands in her lap, and leaned back, her concern showing on her face. Her shoulders sagged, and she looked down at her hands.

"You're laughing because you think my suggestion is foolish," she said.

"No," I said, "I'm laughing because you think I could be angry with you about anything." I put my arm around her shoulders. "I reckon I just need some time to think about your plan."

I stood and took both her hands, pulling her to her feet. We held each other for a while, and then Katie said, "It's late. If I don't go to bed soon, I'm liable to oversleep in the morning. My guests won't be happy if they have to wait for their breakfast."

After we'd said goodnight, I walked to my room. I lit the lamp that sat on a small table, closed the door, and sat on the bed to remove my boots. Without pulling the covers down, I stretched out on my back with my hands behind my head. As I stared at the ceiling, I thought about the conversation I'd had with Katie.

I agreed with her about her second suggestion being better than the first one. I didn't like the idea of leaving her alone while I chased outlaws all over the Arizona Territory. On the other hand, the longer

I thought about taking Katie on the trail with me, even with Wolf riding along, the less I liked the idea.

"What you need, Landry," I said aloud, "is a better suggestion." I reckon I was still trying to think of one when I fell asleep.

I awoke several times during the night from nightmares about Leah coming after Katie and me. Sometimes she and her faceless friend had me tied to a tree while they tortured Katie. One time they tied Katie and me to a stake and set fire to us. Each time I awoke, I had more trouble going back to sleep. I reckon I shouldn't have been surprised when I opened my eyes to sunlight and smelled bacon frying, but I was.

As I pulled on my boots, I noticed the lamp had burned out. Pouring water from a pitcher into a basin, I splashed some of it onto my head and dried myself with the towel that hung from a hook on the wall.

When I closed the door to my room behind me, I heard voices coming from the dining room. The other guests were already enjoying their breakfast. Taking a deep breath, I put on a big smile and stepped around the corner.

"Good morning, Folks," I said. Four of the five guests nodded or waved because their mouths were full.

"Good morning." Katie said. She smiled as she set a plate full of flapjacks on the table in front of Wolf. He was grinning as he moved three of the flapjacks onto his plate.

"Pull up a chair, Brother," he said. "You're missing a delicious breakfast."

We ate without talking. Either because Wolf made them uncomfortable or because they had plans for the day, the other four guests had finished eating and left the table before I poured my second cup of coffee. The last to leave, an elderly couple, excused themselves, wished us a good day, and left the room. Katie was in the kitchen, washing the dishes she had gathered from the table.

"What brought you here?" I asked.

While Wolf chewed a piece of bacon, he stabbed one of the two remaining flapjacks with his fork and slid the plate holding the last one toward me. He washed the bacon down with a swallow of coffee.

"My horse brought me," he said. He was trying not to grin.

"I reckoned we'd meet at my cabin," I said. "I was planning to ride there in a day or two. Why are you grinning?"

Wolf poured some kind of syrup on his flapjack and then handed the small pitcher to me. "Whatever this is," he said, "it makes Katie's good flapjacks taste even better. I'm grinning because you don't look like a man who's planning to ride away from here any time soon."

I poured the rest of the syrup over the flapjack on my plate. "We aren't talking about what I look like," I said. "We're talking about what you're doing here."

Wolf swallowed a mouthful of flapjack and drank some coffee. He was still grinning.

"I'm eating breakfast with my brother," he said, "who doesn't look like a man who's planning to ride away from here any time soon."

I knew Wolf would tell me when he was ready why he had come to Phoenix. I decided to enjoy my breakfast. Wolf was right about the flapjacks tasting good. I reckoned the syrup had to be molasses, although I hadn't tasted it for years.

Wolf finished his meal before I did, but he didn't speak until I had swallowed the last bite of flapjack. Katie walked into the dining room as I poured more coffee into my cup. We thanked her for the meal, and she began to gather the dishes. When I offered to help her carry them, she smiled.

"Thank you," she said, "but I'll get the dishes. I'm sure you two have things to discuss. You can stay here or move to the parlor." She started toward the kitchen, then paused. "I'll join you when I've finished cleaning up."

After Katie had left, I said, "Since you don't seem to want to talk about serious matters, Brother, I'll go first. We have a problem."

Wolf listened without talking while I told him about Leah. When I had finished, he asked, "Are you worried about her and the man who rides with her?"

Katie had left the coffee pot on the table. As Wolf filled his cup, I asked, "Aren't you? Leah is a dangerous woman."

"My people do not worry," he said. "We have work to do. If Leah Fulton tries to stop us, or if she threatens those who are dear to us, we will stop her." He drank some coffee, set his cup on the table, and pulled a folded piece of paper from inside his shirt.

"These people also need to be stopped," he said.

I took the paper and unfolded it. According to the poster, a gang of three men and two women, called "The Players," was wanted for robbery and murder. The reward was $1000, dead or alive. I laid the paper on the table between us and looked at Wolf.

"That's an old poster," he said. "I saw a newer one in Tucson, and the reward was $1500. This gang robbed a stagecoach between here and Yuma two weeks ago."

I slid my empty cup toward Wolf, and he filled it. "How much did they steal?" I asked. "That's a hefty increase in the reward."

"Counting what they took from the passengers," Wolf said, "the stage company reckons they got between a hundred and a hundred fifty dollars."

"And the reward increased by $500?" I asked. "That doesn't make sense."

"It will," Wolf said. He drank some coffee and shook his head. "Brother, before the gang rode away, they shot the driver, the shotgun rider, and the passengers. Two of the passengers were women."

Neither of us spoke while I thought about what Wolf had told me. After a few minutes, I asked, "How does the law know who robbed the stage if the outlaws killed everyone?"

"I said the outlaws *shot* everybody," Wolf said. "The bullet that hit the shotgun rider ricocheted off his gun. He was wounded but still alive when two freighters found him. They patched up as much as they could, loaded him into their wagon, and took him to a doctor in Yuma. He'll be laid up for a spell, but the doc says he'll live."

"You talked to the shotgun rider?" I asked.

Wolf nodded. Katie stopped just inside the doorway to the dining room. Since she had removed her apron, I reckoned she must have finished her work in the kitchen.

"Am I interrupting?" she asked. Wolf and I stood.

"No, Ma'am," I said. "Would you like to join us in the parlor?"

She smiled. "I would!" she said.

Katie and I sat facing Wolf while I repeated what he had told me. She read the poster and handed it back to Wolf.

"According to this," she said, "the gang is already wanted for murder. Do you know anything about their past?"

I shrugged my shoulders and looked at Wolf. "Until I finished my breakfast," I said, "I'd never heard of them."

"I talked to the marshal who gave me this," Wolf said. He folded the poster and slipped it inside his shirt again. "As far as he knows, the gang has been robbing folks for at least three years. During those years, gunplay was only involved one other time."

"And someone was killed?" Katie asked.

Wolf nodded. "According to the marshal," he said, "the gang robbed a stagecoach near Tucson about a year ago."

"They killed everyone?" I asked.

Wolf nodded again. "The driver, the shotgun, and two passengers," he said. Wolf had been leaning back in his chair, but he sat up and leaned forward with his elbows on his knees and his chin resting on his folded hands. "The shotgun rider who was hit by a ricochet told the marshal nobody fired a shot until one of the passengers pulled his gun. While four of the outlaws froze, the fifth one killed the passenger who pulled a gun and then just kept shooting—like someone who'd gone crazy."

Katie and I looked at each other and then at Wolf.

"Did something like that happen during last year's holdup too?" I asked.

"Yep," Wolf said. "One of the passengers, who died later, told the marshal a similar story."

"So, you're saying one man from the gang lost his temper," Katie said, "and killed all those people."

"Nope," Wolf said.

"Are you saying the killer wasn't one of the gang members?" I asked.

"Nope," Wolf said. "The killer was one of the gang members, but the killer wasn't a man."

Chapter 6

W olf, Katie, and I talked until mid-morning. By the time we finished, Wolf and I had decided to leave the next day. Rumor had it the gang was riding toward Prescott. We planned to ride in the same direction until we either caught up with them or learned they were somewhere else.

Wolf left to buy the supplies we'd need while we were on the trail. Katie moved closer to me after we heard the door close behind him. We sat without speaking for a while, and then Katie finally broke the silence.

"I'd rather not be left here alone," she said.

"Can you just lock up here and leave?" I asked.

"Martha said she'd be happy to run this place for as long as I— we need her," Katie said. She smiled, blushed, and took a deep breath. "I told her she could keep half of the money that comes in while we're gone. Since she's a widow too, she can live here until we return—"

She had been watching me as she talked, but she looked at her hands, folded in her lap, and said, "I'm sorry. I can see you really don't want me to come with you. Martha and I can stay here together. If Leah—if anything happens, I'm sure the two of us can handle it."

I wasn't so sure. When she and her friend stopped for the night, Leah couldn't have known I was there too. She couldn't have known Katie was special to me either, but I reckoned she had figured things out pretty quickly after I showed up with her breakfast. Now that she knew Katie mattered to me, Leah would most likely want to kill Katie to make me suffer before she killed me too. I wasn't about to underestimate Leah and put Katie in danger.

"Can you be ready to ride by tomorrow morning?" I asked. When I looked down at Katie, she blinked back tears and smiled.

"I could be ready in an hour," she said. She scooted as close to me as she could get and squeezed my arm again. "Thank you. You won't regret letting me come with you."

Silently I prayed she'd be right.

Since Katie needed to discuss some details with Martha, I excused myself and went to find Wolf. Wolf was rarely predictable, but spending our lives together taught us to share similar thoughts when we did certain tasks. Gathering supplies for the trail was one of those tasks. As I walked down the street, I put myself in Wolf's place. I planned each stop I'd make, and I guessed at how long I'd be there. When I'd finished my calculations, I walked to the livery.

Wolf was checking a pack mule and talking to the livery man as I approached. The man spoke to Wolf. When I was close enough to hear him, Wolf asked, "Fifty dollars?"

I examined the mule, then looked at Wolf.

"He's six or seven years old," Wolf said, "strong and healthy."

I looked at the livery man. "Is a pack saddle included?" I asked.

He pointed toward a rack near the wall. "That one in the middle ain't new," he said, "but it's solid."

"Sold," I said. We shook hands. "We'll need a bill of sale."

The man grinned. "I'll have it ready in a few minutes," he said.

Wolf and I stepped outside to wait. The day was already hot, but we leaned against the front wall of the stable in its shade. A breeze cooled us a little as we watched the townsfolk moving in and out of the shops across the street.

"Did you find everything we need?" I asked.

"Yep," Wolf said, "including these." He pulled two cigars from a leather pouch that hung on a strap draped over his shoulder. He handed one to me, bit the end off the other one, and put the cigar in his mouth.

"I'm obliged," I said. I bit the end off my cigar, pulled a lucifer from my pocket, and lit Wolf's cigar, then mine. For a few minutes, neither of us spoke. Then Wolf broke the silence.

"We're headed for Wickenburg?" he asked.

"I reckon that makes sense," I said. "We might find the gang there."

"Even if we don't," he said, "Dan and Burt may know something that will help us." Wolf took a pull on his cigar and then exhaled a cloud of smoke. "It will be good to see those two again."

"It will" I said. "We should be there in two days. If the gang is there, I reckon we can count on Dan and Burt to help us take them."

The livery man walked out of the stable and handed me a piece of paper. "That pack mule is now legally yours," he said. "I think you'll be happy with her."

I thanked him, glanced at the paper to make sure its contents were accurate, folded it, and tucked it into a vest pocket. After the man had returned to the stable, Wolf continued our conversation.

"If we don't find the gang in Wickenburg," he said, "I reckon we'll ride another two and a half days to Prescott and look for them there."

"We can probably make it to Prescott in two days," I said.

"*We,*" Wolf said, "probably could reach Prescott in two days, but we'll be riding uphill most of the way. We need to think about Katie."

"You're right," I said. "It's not an easy ride; and the higher we get, the harder it is to breathe—wait a minute!" When I looked at Wolf, he was grinning. "I never said anything about Katie coming with us. What makes you think—did Katie tell you she's coming with us?"

Wolf chuckled. "No, my Brother," he said. "Katie *asked* me if she could come with us. She didn't want to cause a problem between you and me by coming if I didn't want her to ride along."

"What did you tell her?" I asked.

"I told her 'yes,' just as you did," he said.

"You want Katie to chase a gang of man-killers with us?" I asked.

Wolf stopped grinning. "Would you rather leave her here without us to protect her?" he asked. "She told me about Leah Fulton and her friend too."

"Why do you think I agreed to let her come with us?" I asked. I dug another lucifer from my pocket, scratched the match on the barn, and re-lit my cigar. "Part of the reason I came looking for you was to ask you what you thought about bringing Katie along."

"Now you know," Wolf said. He took a pull on his cigar, exhaled a cloud of smoke, and watched it disappear as the breeze carried it away. He looked at me. "I hope you already knew."

"I reckon I did," I said, "but I still wanted to ask."

"Huh," Wolf said. He took one last pull on his cigar, dropped the butt on the ground, and stepped on it. After exhaling the smoke, he looked at me. "You plan to leave after breakfast?"

"I do," I said. I dropped my cigar butt and stepped on it. "I don't want to miss having one last breakfast at Katie's place before we leave. You left our supplies at the mercantile?"

Wolf nodded. "We can load the pack mule before breakfast and ride out whenever Katie is ready," he said. "Have you noticed the man across the street who is watching us?"

"The one in the chair who's pretending to sleep?" I asked.

"He was watching and listening in the mercantile while I paid for our supplies and asked the owner if we could pick them up tomorrow morning." Wolf removed his hat, brushed a loose strand of hair away from his face, and replaced the hat. "I wonder why he's interested in us."

I shrugged my shoulders. "We are interesting men," I said. "Maybe he's watching us so he can learn some of the things we know and be like us."

"Maybe," Wolf said, "but I'd feel better if we heard that from him. Should we ask him?"

"I reckon we should," I said.

Wolf and I shook hands as if we were saying goodbye. We separated, walking in opposite directions. As soon as I was sure the watcher couldn't see me, I crossed the street and headed back toward the livery. I knew Wolf would be coming toward me from the opposite direction.

The man still sat in the chair, but he wasn't pretending to be asleep. Instead, he was leaning forward, watching the other side of the street. When he stood, I reckoned he must have decided to follow one of us. A minute later, I knew he'd chosen me.

Turning my back toward the man, I pretended to examine several weapons displayed in the window of the shop closest to where I stood. I slid my Stetson back to let it hang by its stampede string, leaned forward until my nose almost touched the glass, and cupped my hands on both sides of my face as if to block the glare from the sun.

With his attention still focused on the opposite side of the street, the man paid me no mind as he hurried past. I pulled my Stetson on and followed him. When we were a few steps from the next alley, I drew my six-gun and pressed the barrel into his back.

"Turn into the alley," I said, "and keep walking until I tell you to stop. Don't raise your hands but keep them clear of your gun." As we approached the rear of the building, I snatched his six-gun from its holster. "Step behind the building so we can talk."

Wolf was walking toward us along the back of the building. When he stopped a few feet from us, I holstered my six-gun. The man looked younger than Wolf and me by a few years. His clothes were worn but clean; light brown hair stuck out from his battered black hat, and the scraggly hair on his face showed he wasn't shaving yet. I reckoned he was scowling because he was angry with himself for getting caught.

"What's your name, Kid?" I asked.

"I don't have to tell you!" he said. His nostrils flared, and he breathed hard.

"He's right," Wolf said. He looked at the man. "We need to talk to you, and knowing your name might make it easier."

"We could make up a name for him," I said.

Wolf raised his eyebrows and shrugged. "We could," he said. "You pick one."

I studied the man. "Why are you following us, Mary?" I asked.

His face reddened as he snarled at me. "My name's not *Mary!*" he said.

"That's all I have," I said. "I'm sorry, Mary, but—"

"My name is Seth!" he said.

"I reckon," I said, "*Seth* fits you better than *Mary.*" Wolf nodded.

"Why are you following us, Seth?" I asked.

"Can I show you something?" he asked.

"Move slowly and carefully, Seth," I said.

He reached inside his vest, pulled out a folded paper, and handed it to me. When I unfolded it, I was looking at a newer version of the poster Wolf had shown me. This one showed a reward of $1500 for "The Players Gang." I handed it to Wolf, and then I looked at Seth.

"I know who you are, Mr. Landry," he said, "and Mr. Wolf."

"Just Nate," I said, "and just Wolf.

Wolf handed the poster to Seth, who folded it and slipped it back into his vest.

"Why are you carrying this poster around?" Wolf asked.

"I reckon one of you is carrying one just like it," Seth said, "for the same reason I have mine."

Wolf and I looked at each other and then at Seth. "I hope," I said, "you're not thinking about going after this gang."

"If you give me my gun," Seth said, "you'll see how fast I can draw."

"Huh!" Wolf said. "If you brace this gang by yourself, you'll see how fast you can die."

Seth's face reddened. "I never said I planned to go after the gang alone," he said. "I'm looking for the right men to ride with me."

"Well, good luck, Kid," I said. "I hope you find them. "Now, just to be clear, before I give your six-gun back to you, let me ask you again. Why were you following us?"

Seth put his hands on his hips and grinned. "I reckon," he said, "since we're all lookin' to collect the reward on this gang without collecting a bellyful of their lead, we should join up and go after them together."

When Wolf and I didn't reply, Seth's grin faded. He looked surprised, then his face reddened again.

"You two can't take that gang by yourselves!" he said.

"Yes," Wolf replied, "we can."

"You can't stop me from following you!" Seth said.

"We can't," I said. "We won't even try to stop you." I handed Seth his gun, and he shoved it into his holster. "Take care when you're alone on the trail. This bunch were following isn't the only gang in the territory."

"Or the worst," Wolf said.

"I ain't got enough money to tempt an outlaw," Seth said.

"Most of them would shoot you for your horse, your saddle, and your guns," I said. "Some would kill you for your boots."

"You can't scare me," he said.

"We're not trying to scare you," Wolf said. "We're just trying to warn you. Watch your back trail."

Seth was muttering and shaking his head as he disappeared around the corner of the building.

I looked at Wolf. "Were we ever that bullheaded?" I asked.

"You might have been," Wolf said. "My people are not bullheaded. We are sometimes hungry though. Maybe Katie will have food for us."

Chapter 7

---•◦❋◦•---

Katie and Martha had beef sandwiches waiting for us when we walked into her house a while later. As Wolf and I ate, Katie explained she'd need the rest of the afternoon to finish laying out what Martha would have to do while we were gone and answering any questions Martha might have.

"Do you have a guess at how long we might be gone?" Katie asked.

Holding up one finger, I finished chewing a mouthful of sandwich and took a swig of coffee. "Forty days and forty nights," I said.

She rolled her eyes, shook her head, and asked, "Wolf?"

"What Nate means," Wolf said, "is we have no way of knowing how long we'll be gone." He sipped his steaming coffee, set his cup on the table, and shrugged. "If we rode to Prescott, captured the gang the day we arrived, and started back the next day, we'd be gone for close to two weeks."

"If everything went perfectly," I said, "but it rarely does."

"So," Katie said, "we really could be gone for more than a month. I thought you were just trying to be humorous."

"He was," Wolf said. "Are you sure you want to ride with us? I reckon he'll be like this the whole time we're gone."

Katie smiled. "Oh, I'm sure," she said. "I've grown accustomed to his sense of humor."

The ladies had started toward the kitchen when Katie stopped and looked over her shoulder at us. "In fact," she said, "I rather enjoy it—most of the time."

"Huh," Wolf said. "This ride could prove to be harder than I thought it was going to be."

"The hours will rush by," I said.

"At least," Wolf said, "by the time we catch up with the gang, I'll have put up with your sense of humor long enough that I'll be ready to shoot somebody."

"Since Katie and Martha will be busy for a while," I said, "we could talk to the marshal. Maybe he's heard something else about this Players Gang."

As we approached the marshal's office, I spotted him crossing the street. When he saw us, he stopped and waited by the office door.

"Looking for me?" John asked.

"We are," I said. I introduced him to Wolf and told him why we were there.

"Come in," John said. "I may have some news you haven't heard yet."

We sat, John behind his desk, facing Wolf and me. His expression told us his news was bad.

"I received a telegram from the marshal in Wickenburg," he said. "Stop me if you've already heard this. The gang rode through White Tank two days ago, and they robbed some folks who were camped there. The robbery went off without a hitch; but as the outlaws started to ride away, three of the men from the camp grabbed their guns and started shooting. A couple of folks said one of the outlaws was wounded."

"What about the men who tried to stop the gang?" I asked.

"All three are dead," John replied. "Two died where they fell, and the third one died yesterday morning." He removed his hat, laid it on the desk, and ran his fingers through his hair. "A deputy from Wickenburg rode to White Tank and talked to those folks, and most of them said they reckoned the outlaws could have gotten away. When one of them was wounded, another outlaw stopped his horse, turned in his saddle and fired three shots."

John looked at Wolf, then at me. "These are bad men," he said. "Do you think the two of you can stop them?"

"No," I said. "We *know* we can stop them."

John crossed himself. "*Vaya con Dios, mi amigos,*" he said.

When we left the marshal's office, we walked to the mercantile. I bought four cigars and handed two of them to Wolf. He thanked me, and we stepped outside.

I followed Wolf to the last shop that had a bench in front of it. We sat and enjoyed our cigars in silence for a few minutes.

"You think Seth is going to cause problems for us?" I asked.

Wolf took a draw on his cigar and exhaled a cloud of smoke. "He did say he was going to follow us," he said. "I reckoned he meant he'd follow us when we ride out of town in the morning."

"So did I," I said. "He must be afraid we'll sneak out of town when he's not looking."

Seth, who had followed us from the opposite side of the street, stood with his back to us, watching us in a shop window's reflection.

"Wouldn't we have done that by now if we weren't taking Katie along?" Wolf asked.

"We would," I replied. I tapped the ash from the end of my cigar.

"Huh," Wolf said. "I don't expect him to cause problems for us if he keeps his distance." He studied his cigar and then took another draw on it. After letting out another cloud of smoke, he looked at me. "We don't know much about him. He might turn back after a few days, or get lost, or shot by some other outlaw."

"And if he doesn't?" I asked.

Wolf watched Seth and continued to smoke. "He'll need to stay out of our way when we catch up to this gang," he said.

"He'd better," I said, "or he might get us all killed." I took one last draw on my cigar and dropped the butt into a spittoon next to the bench. I stood, stretched, and looked at Wolf. "Reckon we should get to know young Seth a little better—maybe find out what kind of man he is—so we know what to expect on the trail?"

"Yep," Wolf said. He stood, dropped his cigar butt into the spittoon, and grinned. "He might be angry when he finds out we know he's been watching us."

"Let's be friendly so we don't hurt his feelings or embarrass him," I said. As we started across the street, I removed my Stetson, waved it above my head, and yelled, "Howdy, Seth! What've you been looking at for so long in that shop window—your reflection?"

"Why did you do that?" Wolf asked. "Now he'll want to hug you in front of all these folks!"

"He doesn't appear to be in the mood for hugging," I said. Seth, his face red and his right hand close to the butt of his six-gun, spun around to face us as we closed the distance between us. He clenched both hands into fists but opened them as we stepped onto the sidewalk. Wolf and I were smiling, but Seth's expression was far from friendly.

"Wolf and I are headed for that cantina two doors down for some coffee," I said. "Care to join us? We could visit for a spell and get better acquainted."

His nostrils flared, and he replied through gritted teeth. "How stupid do you think I am?"

"Funny you should ask," I said. I was still smiling. "That's just what we're trying to figure out. Come with us; we'll pay for the coffee."

I was pleased to find the cantina almost empty. The five men at the bar glanced at us and then returned to their conversation. Only one table was occupied, and the two men seated at it appeared to be concentrating on their food. Seth followed Wolf and me to a table in a back corner. We took the seats that put our backs against the walls. Seth turned his chair far enough to keep him from sitting with the door directly behind him.

When a thin, gray-haired man came to our table, we ordered coffee. We waited without speaking until he returned with three tin cups and a coffee pot. After filling the cups, he carried the pot to the other table.

"Wolf and I would like to ask you a few questions," I said. "You can answer some, all, or none of them." I sipped my coffee. It was strong and hot, but I'd tasted better. "We're not trying to pry into your business. We'd just like to know what kind of man is going to be following us." I smiled. "When we get to be good enough friends, maybe you could even tell us why you're so dead set on capturing this gang."

"What do you mean?" Seth asked. He tasted his coffee.

"If you're a bounty hunter," Wolf said, "there are plenty of other rewards waiting to be collected. Choosing one of them might mean less money, but it would mean less risk too."

Seth had been holding his cup, and he set it down so hard that coffee splashed onto the table. Both hands were balled into fists.

"I'm not afraid!" he said.

"I'm not talking about being afraid," Wolf said. "I'm talking about being alive."

"Are you a bounty hunter?" I asked.

Seth drank some coffee and then stared into his cup for a while without answering. Finally, he set his cup down and looked at us. "No," he said. After checking to see that no one else was listening, he whispered, "You can't tell anyone about this." Reaching inside his vest, he pulled out a cloth pouch, loosened its drawstring, and emptied its contents into the palm of his left hand. When he tipped his hand toward Wolf and me, we saw Seth was holding a badge.

"Pinkerton's hiring pretty young these days," I said.

"I'm old enough to do my job," Seth said. He dropped the badge into the pouch and tucked the pouch back inside his vest.

When I looked at Wolf, he shrugged. Seth was staring into his cup again.

"How long have you been with the Pinkertons?" I asked.

He glanced around again before holding up three fingers.

"Three years?" I asked.

Without looking at us, Seth shook his head slightly.

"Three *months?*" I asked. When Seth nodded, Wolf let out a quiet "Huh!"

I had been leaning back in my chair, but I sat up and looked at Seth. "How many other cases have you worked?" I asked.

He took a deep breath and let it out slowly, still without looking at Wolf or me. "One," he said.

"One case, and Pinkerton sent you after this gang?" I asked. "You must have really impressed him. Who'd you capture, Frank and Jesse James?"

Seth pushed his chair away from the table and started to stand. "I have things to do."

"Sit down," I said, "and keep talking." To my surprise, he did.

After removing his hat and laying it on the table. Seth ran his fingers through his sandy brown hair. He sat for a few minutes with his elbows on the table and his head cradled in his hands. Finally, he sat straight in his chair, lowered his folded hands to the table, and looked from Wolf to me.

"I failed," he said.

"How?" I asked.

"I was riding the stage from Tucson to Tombstone," he said. "A stagecoach robber was supposed to be one of the passengers, but I failed to discover his identity. The robber had replaced the stage driver, and he escaped with the contents of the strongbox—right under my nose."

The man returned with the coffee pot and filled our cups. We thanked him and waited until he was gone.

"I reckon Mr. Pinkerton wasn't too happy when you reported to him," I said.

"He wasn't," Seth said. "I thought he was going to dismiss me from the Pinkertons. Instead, he told me to work on sharpening my skills. He said he'd contact me when he needed me for another case."

"That sounds promising," Wolf said.

"I thought so too," Seth said, but that was a month ago, and I haven't heard from him."

When I looked at Wolf, I reckoned he was thinking the same thing I was. I sipped my coffee, set my cup down, and leaned back in my chair.

"I hope I'm wrong, Seth," I said, "but I'm guessing you got tired of waiting to hear from Mr. Pinkerton and decided to prove to him you have the makings of a good agent. Bringing in a wanted outlaw or two would show him."

Seth drummed his fingers on the table. "I needed to do something to get me back into the agency!" he said.

"What you're doing," Wolf said, "is more likely to get you into boot hill. Why choose this gang?"

Seth shrugged. "I saw the paper on them," he said, "and I reckoned Mr. Pinkerton would give me another assignment once he saw what I could do."

"You have sand, Kid," I said, "but you seem to be a bit lacking in judgement."

"I told you I was looking for some help," he said. "I didn't reckon on capturing the gang by myself."

I looked at Wolf, and he gave me a nod. "Can you follow orders?" I asked.

Seth looked confused. "I reckon I can," he said. "Why?"

"What if you found a couple of men willing to ride with you, but only if they were in charge?" I asked.

Seth sipped his coffee while he thought. "I don't know," he said. "How would I know I could trust them? They might let me help them catch the gang and then shoot me in the back so they could keep my share of the reward."

"True," Wolf said. "The men you need would not be easy to find. You would have to seek men you could trust. They should be men with experience, men with honor, men with a desire to help you return to work for the Pinkertons."

"Brave men," I said, "men far more intelligent, handsome, and charming than you."

I watched Seth's puzzled expression change to one of understanding as Wolf and I grinned at him. "Wait," he said. "Are you offering to ride with me?" He leaned forward and smiled.

"No, we're not," I said. "We're offering to let you ride with us, but only if you give us your word you'll do as we tell you. Your life — all our lives — could depend on your following orders."

He swallowed hard. "I will do whatever you tell me to do. You have my word."

"Meet us at the livery tomorrow a little before sunup," I said. "If you're not there, the three of us will leave without you."

Seth's grin faded into a confused look. "There's a third man riding with you?" he asked.

"I never said mentioned a third man," I said.

"But you just said—" Seth's face was turning red again. He raised both hands to his shoulders with the palms toward me, took a deep breath, and blew it out of his mouth. Lowering his hands to the table, he began again. "You referred to the *three* of you."

"I did," I said. "Katie Whitman is riding with us. You have a problem with that?"

"I don't like having a woman along on a job like this," he said.

"Neither do we," I said, "but she's coming with us."

"Well then," Seth said. He finished his coffee and stood. "I'll see the three of you in the morning." He had taken three or four steps when he paused, looked back at us, and touched his hat brim. "Thank you, Gentlemen. I won't let you down."

Chapter 8

After supper that night, Wolf sat facing Katie and me in the parlor. Katie listened as I told her about our decision to let Seth ride with us. "How does our plan sound to you?" I asked.

"Wonderful!" Katie said. She smiled at us. "Please don't misunderstand what I'm going to say. I have a lot of faith in you and Wolf, but having Seth come along may help you capture this gang more easily and with less risk. You did say Seth is a Pinkerton agent, didn't you?"

Wolf and I looked at each other and then at Katie. "He showed us his badge," Wolf said.

"Does he have a gun?" Katie asked.

"He does," I said, "and he says he's good with it."

"Do you believe him?" she asked.

"I do," I said. "Wolf?"

"Yes, I believe him," Wolf said. He grinned, and so did I.

Katie looked concerned. What are you not telling me?" she asked. "He has a badge and a gun. You two obviously trust him enough to bring him with us, so what is he lacking?"

We sat in silence for a few minutes before Wolf spoke. "You're much better at explaining things than I am, Brother."

Katie squeezed my hand, and I turned to look at her. "Seth is a good man," I said. "He just doesn't have as much experience as Wolf and I have."

Katie's eyes narrowed. "How old is he?" she asked.

When I looked at Wolf, he shrugged.

"I don't recall his mentioning how old he is," I said.

"How long has he worked for the Pinkertons?" Katie asked.

"Three—maybe four—" I looked at Wolf.

"At least three," Wolf said.

Katie relaxed. "Three or four years of experience is enough to make Seth a reliable man," she said. "Were fortunate to have someone like him to—"

She stood and stepped to one side so she could see Wolf and me at the same time. She put her hands on her hips and asked, "What are you *not* telling me?"

Her expression told me she was sorting through in her mind the information Wolf and I had shared with her. I didn't reckon it would take her long to figure out what was wrong with our story. It took even less time than I thought it would. Katie folded her arms and narrowed her eyes again.

"How long did you say Seth has worked for the Pinkertons?" she asked.

I gave her my most charming smile. "Somewhere between three and four," I said.

Katie wasn't smiling. "Years?" she asked.

I glanced at Wolf. He tried not to grin. "She's talking to you, Brother, not me."

Still smiling, I asked, "What was the question?"

"Nate Landry," she said, "are you telling me you're trusting this man to help us capture a gang of killers when he's only been with the Pinkertons for three or four *months?*"

When I looked at Wolf again, he was staring out the parlor window. "Well," I said, "not exactly."

Katie sat beside me and took my left hand in both of hers. Leaning toward me and looking into my eyes, she asked, "How long has Seth been employed by the Pinkertons?"

"Almost three months," I said.

Katie laid her head on my shoulder and sighed. After a minute or two of silence, she sat up. Still holding my hand, she said, "I don't know enough about Seth to trust him—yet—but I trust you two more than I trust anyone else I know. If you think bringing him along is a good idea, that's good enough for me."

She stood, and so did Wolf and I. "Martha's cooking a good breakfast in the morning," she said. "I'm going to bed. If you gentlemen can find Seth before you turn in, please invite him to join us for breakfast instead of meeting us at the livery. Maybe I can get acquainted with him before we ride out."

Katie hugged Wolf, kissed me goodnight, and left the parlor. Wolf and I walked to the front door.

"Do we know where Seth is staying?" I asked.

"Nope," Wolf replied, "but I'll bet we can find him."

We left the house and walked along the street in the fading daylight. "I hope we're right about trusting Seth," I said. "If we're wrong, there's no telling what that gang will do to us."

"If we're wrong," Wolf said, "we might need to be more concerned about what Katie will do to us."

Something like an hour later, we entered Katie's house, closed the door, and locked it.

"Seth seemed happy about having breakfast with us," I said.

Wolf grinned. "He'll be even happier when he tastes Martha and Katie's cooking," he said. "I'll most likely dream about it tonight."

Katie had lit the lamp in my room before she went to bed. I turned it up as Wolf closed the door. He had been carrying his bedroll under his left arm, and he dropped it on the floor.

"You can have the bed, Brother," I said. "I've been sleeping in it for two weeks. I reckon a night on the floor might help prepare me for the trail."

"I'm obliged," Wolf said. Crouching, he spread his blanket on the floor. "My people," he said, "do not like the white man's soft bed. We sleep better on the ground."

"I figured as much," I said, "but I wanted to make you the offer." I sat on the edge of the bed and pulled my boots off. "Sleep well, and dream about flapjacks."

"Huh!" Wolf said.

I waited until he had stretched out on his bedroll; then I blew out the lamp. I reckon I was thinking about flapjacks—or, at least, Katie cooking flapjacks—when I fell asleep.

When the smell of burning wood awakened me, I first thought Martha and Katie must have built a fire in the stove for cooking breakfast. Then I smelled coal oil and heard the crackling of a fire.

Wolf stood as I pulled on my boots. My moccasins were packed in the saddlebags I had left at the livery.

"Behind the house," Wolf whispered. "Someone's piling brush against the wall!"

The curtains were closed, but I could see the glow of a fire in the darkness. I flung the curtains back and opened the window. Wolf was right. Someone had piled brush against the back of the house, poured coal oil on it, and set it on fire. The flames burned on the far side of the pile, but they were leaping toward the house. They gave off enough light to show two figures disappearing into the darkness.

"We'll deal with them later," Wolf said. "I'll work on the fire if you'll wake the others." He squeezed past me and climbed out the window.

An hour later, Wolf and I stood behind the house with Katie, Martha, and the two guests who had occupied one of her rooms. The young man and his wife, who were expecting their first child, had stopped to rest for a few days before they continued their journey to California. She was crying, and I saw Martha wipe her eyes on her sleeve. Katie's face only showed anger.

The house had hardly been damaged. Instead of trying to fight the fire, we had slipped a discarded telegraph pole between the house and the brush pile. With the help of Seth and a few townsmen who showed up, we had used the pole to scoot the pile far enough away from the house that we could let it burn itself out.

I stood beside Katie with my arm around her shoulder. Leaning toward her, I spoke softly enough that no one else could hear me.

"Did you just growl?" I asked.

"I did," she said. When she looked at me, her face still showed anger. "We could have been killed."

"We're all safe," I said. "Whoever did this has failed."

"They failed this time," she said. She was staring at the brush pile. "I want to find out who did this and—"

"And what?" I asked.

Katie looked at me again. "And make sure they don't try again."

"We'll talk about that on the trail," I said. "For now, let's see if we can get a few more hours of sleep before sunup."

"What?" Katie asked. "How can you go back to sleep after what's happened?"

"I reckon the same way I do every other night," I said. "Will what happened keep you awake?"

At least the anger had disappeared from her face. Instead, she looked confused. Stepping back, she pointed at the smoldering brush pile.

"Somebody tried to kill us," she said. "How do we know they won't wait until we're asleep and then try again?"

"We don't," I said, "but we need sleep. Whoever did this probably lit a shuck out of town right after I opened the window. They won't be back tonight. Even if they do come back, Wolf and I will deal with them." I yawned. "Remember Psalm 4:8, 'I will both lay me down in peace, and sleep: for thou, Lord, only makest me dwell in safety.'"

When Katie moved close and wrapped her arms around me, I could feel her trembling. She was right. We needed to stop whoever had tried to kill us before they tried again. I had no doubt about who it was, and I knew the Dust Devil wouldn't quit.

Chapter 9

⸺⸱•❊•⸱⸺

Nobody was disappointed with breakfast the next morning. Seth had arrived early, and he made no attempt to hide his pleasure as he ate. He was the last one to finish eating. He closed his eyes and smiled as he chewed his final bite of flapjack.

As we stood, each of us thanked the ladies for breakfast. Martha moved to stand beside Seth.

"May I take your plate?" she asked.

"Better hurry," Wolf said, "or he's likely to eat it too."

Martha smiled. "Pay him no mind, Seth," she said. "I enjoy cooking for someone who has a good appetite." She turned toward Katie. "I'll clean this up. You go ahead and get ready to ride."

Seth, Wolf, and I walked to the livery to get the horses and the mule ready while Katie said goodbye to Martha. I knew the fire had left Katie worried about Martha being alone at the house while we were gone. We didn't need her help at the livery, and I reckoned the extra time together might help both women.

Seth helped Wolf load our supplies onto the mule while I saddled Mac and settled our bill with the old livery man. He thanked me and watched as I saddled Katie's horse.

"I hope you found the friends you came here lookin' for," he said.

Mark L. Redmond

I tightened the girth, patted the horse's belly, then checked the girth again. I looked at him over my shoulder as I stroked the horse's neck.

"My friends?" I asked.

"Them two you was hopin' to meet here—a man and a woman," he said.

"You have a good memory," I said. "I'd forgotten I came here. I never did catch up with them."

"Too bad," he said. "It'll be harder now they're gone."

I felt a knot in my stomach. "How do you know they left town?" I asked.

"They rode past here a little more than an hour ago—just after sunup," he said. "A man and a woman I'd never seen before. They seemed to be in a bit of a hurry. I could be mistaken, of course, but they looked like the folks you was hopin' to meet."

"Oh, I reckon we'll meet them somewhere along the trail," I said. I pulled a silver dollar from my vest pocket and handed it to him. "I'm obliged."

When we rode out of Phoenix, the sky was blue, the sun was shining, and a light breeze came from behind us. Wolf and Seth, who was leading the pack mule, rode in front of Katie and me. Birds chirped as they flew overhead or hopped from branch to branch in the scattered trees and brush. Mourning doves surrounded us. We saw a herd of antelope in the distance, and coyotes were everywhere, stealing through the brush to hide in their dens.

"A penny for your thoughts, Mr. Landry," Katie said. "You haven't spoken for at least an hour."

She was riding on my left. When I turned and smiled at her, she took my breath away.

"We should be riding out for a picnic," I said, "instead of tracking a gang of outlaws."

Katie reached to put her hand on mine. "We talked about this. I'm safer here with you than I would be in town alone with Leah after me."

"I need to tell you something I learned about Leah and her friend," I said.

"Is it good news or bad news?" she asked.

"Both," I said. "The good news is that you don't have to worry about Martha or your house because Leah and her friend rode out of town."

"Thank God!" Katie said. She smiled and squeezed my hand. "That's wonderful news!" Her smile faded. "Why did you wait this long to tell me?"

"I didn't want to tell you the rest of it," I said.

"The bad news?" she asked.

I nodded. "I'm pretty sure," I said, "they're somewhere ahead of us, laying an ambush."

Katie hung on to my hand, and we rode without speaking for a while. Still looking straight ahead, she asked, "Do Seth and Wolf know?"

"They do," I said. "I told them right after the livery man told me."

"Do you have a plan to keep them from killing us?" She turned to look at me.

"Find them and kill them first," I said.

"You mean we need to find them and capture them?" she asked. "I know you only kill outlaws when you have to." When I didn't reply, Katie squeezed my hand. "Nate?"

I turned to look at her. "We're after a gang that kills people," I said. "When we catch up to them, they'll try to kill us. Leah and her friend already tried to kill us; and when they get the chance, they'll try again."

Wolf, who had slowed his horse until he rode on the other side of me, heard what I'd just said. When I nodded, he spoke to Katie.

"What my brother is trying to say, Katie," he said, "is the people we're hunting—and the ones who are hunting us—are not the kind of outlaws who will let themselves be captured."

"But you've captured killers before," Katie said. "What makes these outlaws different from the others?"

I knew Wolf was waiting for me to answer, but I looked at him before I spoke. I didn't reckon Katie would like what I had to say.

"The other outlaws," I said, "didn't present a threat to you. The ones we're dealing with now do. I reckon we may have risked our lives a time or two, but we're not going to risk yours."

When Katie didn't look at us or speak for the next mile or so, Wolf and I stayed quiet too. Finally, Katie turned toward us. "Thank you—both of you," she said, "for caring so much about me and for working to keep me safe."

"Hey," Seth said, "is anybody else getting hungry?" He had turned in his saddle and was grinning.

"If we don't stop soon to let him eat," Wolf said, "he might devour the pack mule. I'll ride up there and help him find a place to stop. Our horses could use a little rest."

I looked at Katie and caught her wiping her eyes on her bandana. She turned her head and pretended to look at something in the brush.

"Katie, what's wrong?" I asked.

When she turned toward me, she was crying. "I don't like making your life more difficult," she said.

"You're not making my life more difficult," I said. I held out my hand, and she gave me hers. I raised it to my lips and kissed it. "You're making my life worthwhile."

The day had grown hotter as we rode, and the absence of trees around us made finding some shade a considerable challenge. When Seth and Wolf turned off the trail, I pointed to a dozen boulders about half a mile from us.

"I reckon we'll find shade on the other side of those rocks," I said. "It won't be cool, but we'll be out of the sun for a little while."

"I've gotten spoiled by working inside for so long," Katie said. "I feel as if I'm being baked in my own oven."

I lifted the canteen that hung from my saddle horn, removed the cork, and handed the canteen to Katie. She smiled, took a drink, and handed it back to me. "Thank you, Mr. Landry," she said.

"You're welcome, Mrs. Whitman," I replied.

When we rode around the boulders, Seth was sitting on the ground with his back against the rock. Wolf still sat on his horse.

We often communicated without speaking; so, when Wolf moved his head a little to one side, I understood. I smiled at Katie.

"Get as comfortable as you can," I said, "and cool off a bit. We'll be back."

As we rode away, I was thankful Katie hadn't asked where Wolf and I were headed because I had no idea. I was about to ask Wolf when I saw the buzzards. They were circling something a half mile northeast of us, and most of them were close to the ground.

We rode in silence until we were close enough to see at least twenty buzzards on the ground, feasting on a carcass. Only when we had ridden close enough to scare them off did we realize they had been feeding on *two* carcasses.

"Looks like the horse stepped in a prairie dog hole and broke its leg," I said. "The rider was trapped under it." Our horses were nervous as we circled the grisly scene. I looked at Wolf.

"The rider and the horse were still alive," he said, "when someone took his rifle from its scabbard and rode away."

I dismounted, walked to the man's body, and picked up a canteen that lay on the ground beside him. The cork was missing, and the canteen was empty. So was the exposed saddlebag. I slid my fingers under the canteen, walked back to Wolf, and climbed into Mac's saddle.

"I reckon when this hombre's horse fell, his pardner decided riding double would lessen his own chances of reaching Wickenburg," I said. I took off my Stetson, wiped the sweat from my face with my bandana, and put my hat on again. "He didn't shoot the horse because he didn't want to give away his location. Before he rode away, he took the rifle and emptied the exposed saddlebag. The horse is lying on the other one—and on the rider's six-gun too."

"How long ago?" Wolf asked.

"Less than an hour," I said. "The ground under the canteen is still damp."

"You think the rider was conscious when his pardner rode away?" Wolf asked.

I shook my head. "If he had been, he might have been able to dig out his six-gun and shoot his pardner—or himself. Reckon we should bury him?"

Wolf looked at the buzzards circling above us. "If he was who I think he was," he said, "the buzzards and coyotes can have him."

As we rode toward Seth and Katie, I said, "A person would have to be downright cold-blooded to ride off and leave his pardner to die of thirst in the desert like that."

Wolf looked at me. "Maybe this cold-blooded person rode off and left *her* pardner," he said.

I had been thinking the same thing. Leah Fulton was cold-blooded. She and her companion had been somewhere ahead of us.

When Wolf and I reached the boulders, we found a little more shade than there had been when we left. We were able to crowd all five animals into the shade with us while I told Seth and Katie what we'd found.

"Katie, do you remember what the man with Leah looked like?" I asked. "I know you only saw him briefly."

"He was as tall as you," she said. She took a sip of water from her canteen, closed her eyes, and let her head rest in both hands for a minute. Then she looked at me and continued. "He wasn't dressed like a cowboy. He was wearing a black frock coat, a black vest, striped pants, and a white shirt. He was carrying his hat, so I didn't get a good look at it. Does that help?"

"Yes, Ma'am," I said, "it does."

"Is he the dead man?" she asked.

"I reckon his coat was in the saddlebag under the horse," I said, "but the rest of his outfit matches your description. Looks like the Dust Devil is riding alone."

"What if she runs into the Apaches out there?" Seth asked.

"Huh!" Wolf said. "It could be a bad day for the Apaches."

Chapter 10

·•●⇥⁜⇤●•·

A little before sundown when we stopped to make our camp for the night, the heat forced us to keep our fire small. Seth gathered an armload of brush; Wolf and I took care of the horses and the pack mule, and Katie made coffee and cooked some beans.

We had finished eating and were drinking the last of the coffee when Seth spoke. "I couldn't help but notice we've been riding more to the west than to the north," he said.

"We have," I said. "I'm glad you noticed. It shows you're paying attention."

"Wouldn't riding northwest in a straight line toward Wickenburg get us there faster?" he asked. The look on his face showed his confusion.

"How long since we had rain?" Wolf asked.

Seth thought for a minute. "A month—maybe six weeks," he said.

"At least six weeks," Wolf said. "Long enough for some waterholes to have dried up or had the water level drop too low to be safe for drinking." He nodded toward the canteen beside Seth. "You have enough to last until we get to Wickenburg?"

Seth grinned. "We're riding to the Hassayampa River and then turning north," he said.

I looked at Wolf. "There's hope for this young fella," I said.

"Yep," Wolf said. He was looking at Seth. "By riding west, we'll also be keeping our distance from Leah Fulton."

"Are you two afraid of a woman?" Seth asked.

Wolf and I looked at each other. "Not afraid," I said, "but aware of what she is. She's as capable of killing us as any man we've ever hunted was."

"More capable than some," Wolf said. "Think of her the way you'd think of a rattlesnake. You don't need to fear it, but you need to be careful when you're around it."

"She's one of the reasons we'll take turns standing guard tonight," I said.

Seth had stopped grinning. "What do you mean, *one* of the reasons?" he asked.

"Didn't the Pinkertons teach you about the Apaches?" I asked.

"Of course they did," he said, "but we haven't seen any today!"

Wolf and I both laughed. "You only see an Apache," Wolf said, "when he wants you to see him. This is their territory."

"Do you think they're near here?" Katie asked.

"I reckon they've been watching us all day," I said. When Katie moved closer to me, I felt her shiver.

Wolf was watching her. "If we leave them alone," he said, "most of them will leave us alone as well."

"You said *most* of them," Seth said. "What if some of them are looking for trouble?"

"We'll show them where to find it," Wolf said, "just as we would show white men who were looking for trouble."

Since Wolf had the first watch, Seth, Katie, and I spread our bedrolls. I carried Katie's saddle to her and laid it at the head of her blanket.

"It's not the best pillow," I said, "but it's the best one we have."

I laid my saddle at one end of my blanket and sat at the other end. I removed my boots, pulled on my moccasins, and stretched out on my back. Katie lay less than six feet from me on my left; and Seth was twice as far away on my right, closer to our horses. Reaching out in the semi-darkness, I took Katie's hand in mine.

"Sweet dreams," I said.

"Thank you, Mr. Landry," Wolf replied.

"Shut up, you crazy Indian," I said.

I fell asleep and dreamed that Leah Fulton was chasing Katie and me across the desert. Leah was riding a horse, but Katie and I were on foot. When Katie stumbled and fell, Leah tied her hands and feet, piled brush on top of Katie, and was getting ready to set fire to it. I grabbed her wrist from behind to stop her, and she turned to face me. With her snarling face inches from mine, Leah grabbed my shoulder with her free hand and tried to push me away.

I awoke to find the hand on my shoulder was Wolf's. I could see his silhouette as he crouched beside me.

"Your watch," he whispered. "All is quiet."

The night was cool, but the rocks still held some of the heat they had absorbed during the day. I leaned against one of the bigger ones and listened for any sound that was out of place. The desert came alive at night, playing its own special music. When I heard a sound coming from our camp, I turned toward it and watched Katie appear from the darkness. She had wrapped herself in her blanket; and when she saw me, she walked over and snuggled against me. I put my arm around her shoulders and pulled her closer.

"I thought I was supposed to stand guard," I said, "and you were supposed to sleep."

"I slept until Wolf came to get you," she said, "and I'll probably sleep again while Seth stands guard."

"You can't sleep while I'm on guard?" I asked. "Don't you trust me?"

Katie laid her head on my shoulder. "I trust you," she said, "more than I trust any other man I know. I also love you, and I didn't want you to be out here alone."

I leaned away from her and looked down at her upturned face. "Well. That's mighty neighborly of you, Ma'am," I said.

She raised herself on her tiptoes and kissed me. "I'm a mighty neighborly person, Mister," she said.

We listened to the night sounds, admired the stars, and talked. The hours passed too quickly; and then it was time to wake Seth.

Katie and I watched him buckle his gun belt on and disappear into the darkness. As we turned to face each other, I took her hands in mine and gently pulled her closer to me.

"I still don't like having you out in open country like this," I said, "but I reckon your being here does have a good side to it."

"What is it?" Katie asked. She was looking up at me; and although I couldn't see her expression, I knew she was smiling.

"I get to kiss you goodnight twice," I said.

"I only remember you kissing me goodnight once, Mr. Landry," she said.

Neither of us spoke for the next few minutes. I ended the silence with a question.

"What do you remember now, Mrs. Whitman?" I asked. Katie sighed and hugged me.

We said goodnight and stretched out on our bedrolls. I don't know who fell asleep first, but it didn't take long for either of us.

In the morning, we had coffee and beans before we rode away from our camp. The sun rose, bringing plenty of heat with it. We rode in silence for an hour, watching in every direction for anything out of place. I saw plenty of movement from the critters that lived in the desert. Some were hunting for their breakfast; others *were* breakfast.

Wolf and I were used to seeing these critters, but many of them were new to Katie and Seth. I heard Katie gasp.

"Is that a cougar?" she asked. I looked in the direction she was pointing and smiled.

"It's a bobcat," I said.

"Is it dangerous?" she asked. She reined her horse closer to Mac.

"Only if you're a kangaroo rat," I said, "or a ground squirrel, quail, jackrabbit, snake, or maybe a lizard. I don't reckon it will bother us"

"I've seen fourteen coyotes so far," Seth said. "Have you gents ever seen that many in such a short time?"

Since Seth was riding behind me, I knew he couldn't see my smile when I replied.

"Don't know," I said.

"What?" Seth asked. "What's the highest number of coyotes you've ever seen in—let's say—an hour?"

"I have no idea," I said. "Wolf?" I knew Seth was looking at Wolf, waiting for his answer.

"Coyotes are everywhere," Wolf said. "We have no reason to count them, but fourteen is a lot of coyotes."

Another hour had passed before Seth spoke to us. By the time we stopped to rest, he was friendly again.

We had found an outcropping that provided enough shade for us and our mounts with room to spare. We sat on the ground, eating jerky and hardtack.

"I know we won't reach the river today," Katie said, "but how far will we need to travel tomorrow?"

Since I had a mouthful of jerky, I nodded at Wolf.

"We should reach the river before sundown," he said, "if we have no delays."

"Like trouble with Apaches or Leah Fulton?" Seth asked.

"Those are two of the possible reasons for being delayed," Wolf said, "but not the only two."

"Did we forget to mention how much fun you can have on the trail when you ride with us?" I asked.

Seth drank a little water and looked from Wolf to me. "I reckon you left out that part," he said, "but I can handle a little fun once in a while."

The remainder of the day and that night passed as peacefully as the previous one had, and sunup the next morning found us headed toward the Hassayampa River. Our supply of water was beginning to run low, but we still had enough to get us to the river.

Wolf and I watched in every direction as we rode, and I hoped Katie and Seth were watching too. I knew Wolf, like me, was also alert to every scent and sound around us. I was almost surprised we'd had no "delays" when we stopped to rest at midday.

"Once we reach the Hassayampa River," Katie said, "we'll still have at least a half day's ride to Wickenburg. Am I correct?" She bit the end off a strip of jerky.

"Close enough," I said.

"Do you reckon whoever is following us will come at us tonight or tomorrow?" she asked.

After I had finished choking on a mouthful of water. I turned to look at Katie. She sat on the ground beside me, smiling like a mischievous little girl.

"When did you spot them?" I asked.

"I didn't," she replied.

"Then how did you know—"

"I'm not as good as you and Wolf are at reading the signs around me," she said. "Since I can read you and Wolf well enough to know when something's wrong, I've just been watching you."

"Knowing that you can read me that well," I said, "almost scares me."

Katie smiled. "Do I scare you more than Leah Fulton does?" she asked.

I thought about her question for a minute before I replied. "She may be a little cleverer than you," I said.

"Really?" Katie asked. "What makes you think I'm not just as clever as she is?"

I turned toward her and smiled. "No offense, Ma'am," I said, "but she's out there somewhere, and we don't know where; but I caught you."

Chapter 11

----•◦❈◦•----

As usual, Wolf had been right. When we dismounted near the east bank of the Hassayampa River, we still had at least two hours of daylight left. We filled our canteens first, drank as much as we wanted, and then topped them off. While the horses quenched their thirst, we filled the goatskin bag and the spare canteen from the pack mule.

Wolf glanced at the sky and then looked at me. Katie swung into her saddle. She was smiling at all three of us.

"What are you doing?" I asked.

"I saw the look Wolf just gave you," she said, "and your response. You'd like to keep riding instead of burning daylight, but you're concerned about me. You needn't be. Let's ride!"

"Huh!" Wolf said. "My people do not fear women, but Katie *is* a little scary."

"She is, Brother," I said. "It's a good thing she likes us."

As we mounted our horses, Seth asked, "Do you think she likes me too?"

"You'd best hope she does," I said. The look on Seth's face made me grin. "I reckon you're safe."

Wolf had first watch that night. As soon as I was sure both Seth and Katie were asleep, I left my bedroll and found him. We stood without speaking for a while, looking at the stars and listening to the night music of the Hassayampa.

"This gang of play-actors," I said, "could still be in Wickenburg."

"They could," Wolf said. "Do we have a plan?"

"I have an idea," I said, "but I need to know what you think of it."

Wolf listened as I explained my idea. When I had finished, he remained quiet for a few minutes. A fish splashed in the river.

"Your plan is good," he said. "If this gang is not in Wickenburg, it should still work in Prescott. Wickenburg would be better for us because Dan and Burt will help."

We talked about other things for a while. Finally, Wolf said, "You should get some sleep, Brother. We can talk more tomorrow."

A few minutes later, I lay on my bedroll, looking at the stars. I thought about the outlaws we were tracking. At least one of them was a cold-blooded killer. Wolf and I needed to capture or kill that man while we protected Katie from him and the rest of the gang. I reckoned my idea for catching them was as good as any other; I just hoped it would prove to be good enough.

I was awake for a while. When I finally fell asleep, I was asking God for His help.

What seemed like a few minutes later, Wolf awakened me. "Someone is watching," he whispered, "but just watching."

As soon as I left the camp, I understood what had warned Wolf of someone's presence. The river music had paused. After a few minutes of silence, it began again, then paused again. In the darkness, someone I couldn't see was moving. The night critters saw him; they always knew when someone was close. Whoever it was must be moving up and down the river because the music continued to start and stop. Either Wolf or I would have heard him if he had been moving through the brush.

I reckoned Wolf was right about whoever was out there not being a threat to us—at least, not for now. I wondered what would happen at sunup. I also wondered who was watching us. As far as we knew, the Players Gang wasn't aware that we were on their trail. Although Leah Fulton was hunting us, I couldn't imagine she'd be stalking us in the darkness. That left the Apaches, and they might be watching us to see what we were up to. We'd likely find out in the morning.

The rest of my watch was quiet except for the night music, which only stopped one more time. When my watch duty was finished, I woke Seth, lay on my bedroll, and fell asleep.

I opened my eyes just before sunup. Either Wolf or Seth had built a small fire, and I could smell coffee. They stood a little beyond the fire, talking quietly. When I joined them, both men turned toward me.

"Do we have company this morning?" I asked.

"Whoever was here last night," Wolf said, "is gone now."

"Good," I said. "Since that leaves you two unoccupied, I'd like some biscuits and gravy for breakfast, please."

Seth looked at Wolf, then grinned at me. "I reckon you'd best go back to sleep then, Pardner," he said, "because the only place you'll find that breakfast this morning is in your dreams."

I settled for beans and hardtack instead of biscuits and gravy. At least the company was good. As soon as we had finished our breakfast, we put out the fire, saddled up, and headed toward Wickenburg.

As we rode, Wolf and Seth pulled up next to Katie and me. We rode in silence for a few minutes, but then Wolf spoke.

"I reckon you should tell Seth and Katie what we plan to do when we reach Wickenburg," he said. "They may think of something we have overlooked."

Katie smiled, and Seth shook his head. He removed his hat, ran his fingers through his hair, and wiped his sweaty hand with his bandana. Then he chuckled.

"I can't imagine you two overlooking anything," he said. "If you ever did though, do you really believe I might notice it?"

"I reckon it's possible," I said. "It might even be likely. Let's find out."

"One reason these outlaws have been successful is their intelligence." I took a long drink from my canteen. "As far as we know, there are five people in the gang; and at least one of them is a woman. Somewhere along the way, these outlaws learned that most folks only notice things they're expecting to see."

"I don't follow you," Seth said.

"Wolf and I had a friend during the war who always wore a full beard," I said. "After the war had ended, he shaved it off. When he returned from the creek where he'd gone to shave, nobody recognized him. They had been expecting to see a man with a full beard."

"I understand your point," Katie said, "but what does it have to do with this "Players Gang?"

The wind was getting stronger. I tightened the stampede string on my Stetson and smiled at her. Then I turned toward Seth.

"Tell me how you think a gang of outlaws would rob a bank," I said.

"Jesse James and his gang," Seth said, "would drift into a town from both ends and hitch their horses near the bank. They'd wear masks, and three or four of the men would enter the bank with their guns drawn while the rest held the horses and watched the street."

"And after they got the money?" I asked.

"They'd light a shuck out of town and get as far away as possible before the townsfolk could put a posse together," Seth said. "They'd probably have fresh horses waiting somewhere along the trail."

"I reckon that's the description most lawmen, most bounty hunters, and most Pinkerton agents would give," I said. "It's also the reason this gang hasn't been caught yet."

"Now you've really lost me," Seth said. He removed his bandana, wiped his face and neck, and then held one corner of the bandana to let it dry in the wind. "What is this gang doing that's different?"

"For one thing," I said, "these outlaws are wearing a different kind of mask." I took a drink of warm water from my canteen. "Think about it. At least two of them are most likely thespians."

"What's a thespian?" Seth asked.

"An actor," Katie said.

"Well, why didn't he just say so?" Seth asked.

"Sorry," I said. "Think about the way a man's appearance changes when he shaves off a full beard. What if a clean-shaven man *put on* a full beard?"

"What if a *woman* put on a full beard and a man's clothes?" Katie asked. "If she left town, removed the beard, changed into a dress, and climbed into a buckboard left there earlier, a posse pursuing outlaws would ride past her without giving her a second look."

"Pinkerton agents often use disguises," Seth said. "So, the lady hides one outlaw under a tarp in her buckboard. The posse hears a few shots, and soon they find two riders. One is on the ground, bleeding from a wound in his shoulder, and the other is doctoring the wound. He waves away any offer of help, telling the posse members his friend's wound isn't bad and urging them to catch the outlaws."

"The fifth man," Katie said, "is sitting on the ground, and he's dressed like a farmer. He's holding the reins to his horse, but he tells the posse the outlaws took his fresh horse at gunpoint and left their tired horse with him!"

"Yep," Wolf said. "They understand. It's a good thing they're not outlaws. They seem to have caught on quickly to some of the ways to fool a posse." He swatted a horsefly that had been buzzing around his head. "Now you can tell them your plan."

"Even if we knew what the outlaws look like," I said, "we wouldn't recognize them once they've disguised themselves."

"Well, I don't know about you, Katie," Seth said, "but that thought makes me feel better."

"Hold on, Seth," I said. "I'm not finished. They don't know who we are either. They could still be in Wickenburg. If Katie and I ride into town from the south, but you and Wolf ride in from the north just before sundown, we won't be as likely to raise their suspicions. Wolf and I can talk to Dan and Burt to see what they know. How does that sound to you two?"

"What if the gang has already ridden out of Wickenburg?" Seth asked.

"We'll try the same thing again when we reach Prescott," I said.

Seth shrugged his shoulders. "Can't hurt to try," he said. "I sure don't have a better idea than this one."

When I looked at Katie, she nodded. "We'll beat these outlaws at their own game," she said.

"I reckon we will," I replied.

"We'll take the pack mule with us," Wolf said, "so you won't have to bother with it when you get to town." He turned toward Seth. "We're close enough to Wickenburg to start around it. We can take our time and ride into town close to sundown. We might even wait until morning."

As they rode east, Katie and I continued toward town. She wiped her face and neck with a handkerchief.

"We're almost there, aren't we?" she asked.

"Yes, Ma'am," I said.

"Are you afraid?" she asked.

"Of what?" I was grinning, and I laughed when she gave my arm a playful punch.

"I'm alert," I said, "and I'm cautious." I looked at Katie. "We have an edge that will help us defeat this gang no matter where we find them."

"We have God on our side," she said.

"Psalm 27:1-3 always calms me at times like this," I said. "'The Lord is the stronghold of my life—of whom shall I be afraid? When evil men advance against me to devour my flesh, when my enemies and my foes attack me, they will stumble and fall. Though an army besiege me, my heart will not fear; though war break out against me, even then will I be confident.' It's not an exact quote, but the meaning is the same."

She guided her horse closer to Mac and leaned toward me. We halted our horses while we kissed. As we started forward again, Katie was smiling.

"Thank you, Nate," she said.

"For what?" I asked.

Katie sighed. "For being the best man I've ever known," she said, "for loving me, for letting me love you—"

I didn't have to look at her to know she was crying. "I reckon I'm the one who should be obliged," I said.

Chapter 12

———•◦→✦←◦•———

Although I hadn't seen Wickenburg for close to a year, everything seemed familiar to me as Katie and I rode into town. I needed to avoid being recognized by the few townsfolk who might remember me as a bounty hunter. I hoped my being accompanied by Katie instead of Wolf would help me succeed.

Both of us were hungry, but Katie wanted to take a bath before we ate. I reckoned I needed to bathe too since I would be spending time with Katie and other folks who might object to the way I smelled.

We tied our horses to the rail in front of a boarding house and went inside. The short, thin, gray-haired lady behind the counter smiled as she told us she had the two rooms we needed as well as two separate rooms for bathing. She led us to our rooms and pointed toward the end of the hallway.

"I'll have water in both tubs if you can give me half an hour," she said. "The tub in the room on the right is larger than the other one." She turned and hurried back toward the counter.

"Oh, no!" Katie said.

I had opened the door to my room, which was across the hall from Katie's; but I turned toward her when she spoke. She was obviously upset.

"What's wrong?" I asked. She looked as if she was about to cry.

"I packed clean clothing because I didn't want to wander through Wickenburg dressed like a man!"

90

I had no idea about what—if anything—I was supposed to say. I stood there, smiling at Katie, waiting for her to enlighten me. When she let out a long sigh but didn't speak, I decided to risk a question.

"Did you bring them?" I asked.

"Yes, I did," she replied. Her face reddened. Now I was really confused.

"Isn't that a good thing?" I asked.

Katie's smile didn't reach her eyes. "It would be," she said, "if Seth and Wolf were here with the pack mule."

"What can I do to help?" I asked. When Katie's smile reached her eyes, I had a feeling I wouldn't like what came next. As it turned out, I was right.

Katie gave me detailed instructions. About the time she started her bath, I was buying a dress at the closest mercantile. When I told the storekeeper what I wanted, he called his wife to help me.

"I need to buy a dress, Ma'am," I said.

"What size?" she asked.

"About the same size you wear, Ma'am," I said.

She smiled as she showed me three calico dresses.

"I'd like the blue one, please," I said, "and the pink one, too—just in case she doesn't like the first one."

"How wonderful to wait on a man who's so attentive to his wife!" she said.

"She's not my wife," I said. The lady's smile turned to a look of disgust.

"Oh," she said. "I see."

My face felt hot, and I knew I was blushing. "No—it's not what you think, Ma'am," I said. "She's at the boarding house up the street, taking a bath—"

She raised her hand to her throat. "Really!" she said. "I think you've said enough, young man!" She stomped to the counter and threw the dresses on it. "Take this heathen's money, and get him out of here," she said.

I looked at the storekeeper and shrugged my shoulders. He grinned.

"These won't fit you," he said. "Next time you might consider buying the fabric and making the dresses yourself."

"I'm obliged," I said. "I usually make my own, but I'm a little pressed for time this week." I tugged the brim of my hat, turned, and walked out of the mercantile.

Back at the boarding house, I tapped on the door to Katie's room. When no one responded, I reckoned Katie must still be taking her bath. The door was unlocked. I stepped into her room and laid the dresses on her bed. Pulling the door closed behind me, I hurried to my room.

I reckoned I must have been gone for half an hour. We were both hungry, and I didn't want Katie to have to wait while I finished my bath. In the second bathroom, I washed quickly, dried on the towel the hotel had provided, and pulled on the only other union suit I owned. Since I had emptied my pockets in my room, I dropped my dirty union suit, shirt, and bandana into the tub and scrubbed them too. I needed to put the only pair of pants I'd brought with me on again, so I'd have to wash them later.

Back in my room, I hung my wet shirt over the only chair and my union suit on a hook someone had fastened to the wall. I draped my bandana over the unlit lamp that sat on a small table. I pulled on and buttoned my clean shirt, then tied my clean bandana around my neck.

Pleased with myself for not making Katie wait, I opened my door to check the hallway. It was empty. Smiling, I had started to close the door when I heard a splash and the sound of a woman singing softly. It was coming from the room where Katie was supposed to take her bath. As I listened, I recognized Katie's voice. She was still in the water.

My stomach growled. I had forgotten how much time a woman sometimes needed to prepare herself for being seen in public places. The midday meal I thought we would eat together was beginning to look more like supper.

I put on my Stetson, buckled on my six-gun, and left the boarding house. In the hallway I met a girl who carried a large, tin pail full of steaming water. Watching over my shoulder, I saw her knock at the door of the room where Katie was. I hoped we'd be dining before dark.

I walked into the first cantina I came to. Since it was the time of day when folks who didn't have to take a bath usually ate their midday meal, every table was occupied, and the bar was crowded. Three or four people were seated at most of the tables. I bought a beer, helped myself to a sandwich and a pickled egg, and walked to a corner table where a priest sat alone.

"Would you object to some company?" I asked.

The priest looked up at me and smiled. He gestured toward the three empty chairs.

"You are welcome, my Friend," he said. "Not many people wish to break bread with a priest."

"Well, I don't mind sharing your table," I said. "I'm obliged for the seat."

"You are new in town?" he asked. He was eating the same food I was, and he bit into his half-eaten sandwich.

I had taken a bite of my egg, and I chewed it, swallowed it, and tasted my beer before I replied.

"Just passing through," I said.

"We are all just passing through," he said.

"We ate in silence for a while, and I studied him. He had a round, friendly face, tan skin, brown eyes, and long, slender fingers. The little finger on his left hand was missing almost an inch of its tip.

"Forgive my lack of manners," he said. "I am Father Barnabas."

"Pleasure to meet you," I said. "I'm Nate Jackson." I took another bite of my sandwich. The bread was a little dry, but the thin slices of beef were good. I was hungrier than I had realized.

"What—if you don't mind my asking—do you do for a living, Mr. Jackson?" he asked. He put the last bite of his sandwich into his mouth and chewed it while he wrapped both hands around his glass of beer. When he had finished chewing, he swallowed, then took a drink.

"I've done a little bit of everything that needed doing, I reckon," I said. "Since the war ended, I've been drifting around the Arizona Territory. I'm not afraid of hard work, but I haven't found a place where I want to put down roots yet."

He took another drink and set his glass on the table again. Looking at the glass, he shook his head slowly and smiled.

"I did my share of drifting when I was your age," he said. He looked at me, still smiling. "Will you stay in Wickenburg long, or are you passing through in a hurry?"

He must have seen in my expression the curiosity I was feeling. He chuckled.

"Forgive me," he said. "Most of my conversations with people take place in the confessional. I don't often get a chance to simply talk with another person. You must think you are breaking bread with the town gossip."

"No offense taken, Father Barnabas," I said. I finished my sandwich and drank the last of my beer. "I'm not sure how long I'll be here. I intend to see if anyone has work for me. If I find some, I'll stay for a spell. If not, I'll ride out tomorrow or the next day."

I stood and pushed my chair against the table. "Thank you for the chair and the conversation," I said. "Perhaps we'll meet again."

"I hope we do," he said.

As I walked back toward the boarding house, I was still hungry. I had wanted to eat another sandwich, but I reckoned Katie would notice if I wasn't very hungry at supper. I checked the bathing room first, and I was relieved to find the door ajar. Katie's not still being in the bathtub brought me some hope that we might dine before sundown.

My experience with women preparing to go out was limited. Although Elizabeth and I had been married for almost two years, our trips away from the ranch had consisted of driving our buckboard eight miles to town for supplies twice each month. Spending much time to prepare for a ride that left folks covered in dust would have been plumb crazy.

I went to my room and rolled up my dry bandana, shirt, and union suit before tucking them into one of my saddlebags. After pulling the chair next to the window, I sat down to think while I watched the townsfolk on the street.

I wanted to find Dan or Burt to let them know we were in town. I also wanted to find out if they knew anything about the Players Gang that we didn't. It was still early afternoon. I reckoned I could knock on Katie's door and ask her how much more time she needed to get ready for supper. I decided not to do that because, being the sweet, thoughtful woman she was, she would hurry to finish her preparations just to avoid making me wait for her. I wanted Katie to take her time and to recover a bit from what she'd gone through in the past week.

I could avoid rushing Katie if I just slipped out of the hotel again to look for Dan and Burt. If I hadn't returned by the time Katie was ready to go, she would be worried that something had happened to me. I couldn't put her through that either.

I took the only action left to me. I stayed in the chair and watched the street from my window. I had opened both the window and the door to allow the breeze free passage through my room, but I still used my bandana to wipe my face and neck every few minutes.

During the first half hour or so, I saw a few folks I recognized from the previous visit Wolf and I had made to Wickenburg. Tired from the nights on the trail, I began to doze for a few minutes at a time. Finally, because I didn't want to miss Dan or Burt, I stood for a while.

When Father Barnabas walked past my window, I was surprised to see him accompanied by a saloon girl. They appeared to be having a serious conversation. As they moved out of sight, I smiled. "He keeps company with some of the same kind of folks Jesus did," I said.

During the next quarter of an hour, I recognized three more people I had met on my previous visit. I had just sat down again when Dan and Burt strolled into sight, headed toward the marshal's office.

I left the boarding house and started walking in the same direction the lawmen had gone. I turned into the first alley I saw and moved to the back of the buildings. Seeing no one in either direction, I hurried along behind the buildings until I reached the back door to the marshal's office. I knocked, waited a minute, and knocked again. I smiled when I heard Burt grumbling as he slid the bolt and swung the door open.

"Most folks use the front door," he said, "instead of skulking around back here like a—" he stood in the doorway with his mouth open and blinked his eyes twice. "Nate Landry, is that you?"

"It was when I got up this morning," I said. "Are you going to let me in, you cantankerous old man, or are you just going to stand there and watch the sun bake me?"

We both laughed as we shook hands. Holding a finger to his lips, he closed the door and slid the bolt into place. I followed him down a short hallway and into the office, where Dan sat at his desk. We stood behind him, and he spoke without turning to look at us.

"Why did somebody think using the back door was a good idea?" he asked.

"I reckon," I said, "some folks don't want to tarnish their good reputation by being seen with a couple of hombres like you."

Dan was already grinning when he stood and turned to face me. Gripping my shoulder with his left hand, he shook my right and chuckled.

"Good to see you again," he said. "What brings you to Wickenburg—business or pleasure?"

"A little of both, I reckon," I said, "but right now I only have time to talk business."

The two lawmen listened while I told them what I knew about the gang.

"We've heard about them," Burt said, "but we didn't know they were headed in our direction." He removed his hat and scratched his head. "I reckon we'd have noticed—or at least, heard about five strangers riding into town, even if they rode in at night."

"They wouldn't have ridden in together," I said. "They would ride into town from different directions—probably on different days—to keep from drawing attention to themselves. Also, one of them was shot while riding away from their last job. Nobody knows how badly he was wounded."

"You're not going to tell us about the pleasure, are you?" Dan asked. He was grinning. "Not even a hint?"

"I'll tell you later," I said. "I'm having supper with someone, and I don't want to be late." I started toward the back door.

"What time will you be eating?" Burt asked.

I paused and looked over my shoulder at them. I couldn't help but grin.

"I have no idea," I said, "but I am looking forward to a pleasant experience."

"Burt and I will make a list of strangers in town," Dan said. "I reckon we might start with you." They were laughing as I closed the door behind me.

Chapter 13

The sandwich I had eaten earlier was a good one, but it hadn't been enough to keep me from being hungry as I walked back to the boarding house. As I sat in my room, I started to wish I had eaten a second sandwich. I had been lying on my back for a few minutes, listening to my stomach complain, when someone knocked on my door. When I opened it, Kate stood there, wearing the blue dress. Every minute I'd spent keeping myself occupied had been worth the wait.

"I'm sorry I took so long to get ready," Katie said. "I usually take half the time I took today, but I felt so dirty—my hair was a mess—and I—"

I put my arms around her, pulled her close, and kissed her. When the kiss ended, I kept my hands on her shoulders and held her at arm's length.

"You take my breath away, Katie," I said. Pulling the door closed behind me, I offered her my arm. "Would you do me the honor of having supper with me, Ma'am?"

She hugged my arm as we started down the hall. "I will, Sir," she said, "but the honor, I believe, will be mine."

We ate supper at an eating place the owner of the boarding house had recommended. The food was supposed to be good; and the place was busy, but not crowded. We both ordered steak, potatoes, and beans. When a young lady brought our food, each plate also held a thick slice of buttered bread. The same young lady filled our cups with steaming coffee.

When I told Katie about my visit with Dan and Burt, she was happy to hear I'd found them. Her smile faded when I mentioned their lack of knowledge about the gang.

"How will we know if the gang is still in Wickenburg?" she asked. As she tasted her bread, her eyes widened. She held the slice in one hand and pointed at it with the other. "This is delicious!"

"We'll have to look around," I said, "for anyone who doesn't fit in." I took a bite of my steak.

"But if these people are good actors," Katie said, "they *will* fit in." She stirred the beans on her plate with her fork.

The young lady stopped at our table and refilled our cups. Katie smiled and thanked her. "Where do you get your bread?" she asked.

The lady returned Katie's smile. "It's the best I've ever tasted!" she said. "Our new cook bakes it himself, but he won't share his recipe." As she moved to the next table, Katie and I stopped eating and looked at each other.

"You're right," I said. "They'll fit in. They'll also be new at their jobs."

"Like the cook?" Katie asked. Her eyes sparkled.

"Like the cook," I said, "maybe." I bit off a chunk of bread and chewed it. Katie was right; the bread was delicious.

"What do we do next?" she asked. Her eyes still sparkled.

"We find Wolf and Seth," I said. I drank some coffee. It was still plenty hot. "Or they find us. We need to talk to Dan and Burt together with Wolf and Seth, but we'll have to meet in secret."

"When?" Katie asked. She slid her plate to one side and leaned forward, her forearms resting on the table. I tried not to smile.

"I reckon tonight would be good," I said. "We just need to sort out where to meet and how to get word to the others."

Katie slid her plate back to where it had been and started eating again. Neither of us spoke for the next few minutes. I was chewing the last bite of my steak when Katie giggled. I finished the meat and sipped my coffee.

"Are you going to tell me what's so funny, or do I have to guess?" I asked.

"You're the best man I know," she said, "but I think you need to go to jail."

I smiled. "If you mean Dan's office," I said, "and we can get word to Wolf and Seth, we can use the back door. No one will know we're there."

I paid for our food, and we left the eating place. After discussing several possible plans, Katie and I had decided to ride out of town together. Anyone who took notice would just see a man and woman taking a romantic ride. I reckoned that's just what we were doing. We were also looking for the place where our friends were camped.

As we rode out of town, Katie asked, "Did you recognize the livery man? He didn't seem to remember you from your last visit."

I smiled. "You reckon he's new in town?" I asked.

"I've been thinking," she said. "If you and I wanted to try to do what these players have been doing, what roles would we choose?"

"What do you mean?" I asked.

Katie swatted at a fly that seemed determined to land on her face. She looked at me.

"Would you pretend to be a lawyer or a politician?" she asked. "What about a singer or an artist?"

"Ah," I said, "I catch your drift." I gave her one of my most charming smiles. Katie showed her incredible strength by not falling from her saddle. "You believe these outlaws would choose to become folks nobody would notice—like 'the butcher, the baker, the candlestick maker'!"

"Wouldn't you?" Katie asked, "especially if you weren't one of the better actors in the gang? You'd want to attract as little attention as possible." Her eyes were sparkling again. "Who pays attention to the people who do menial tasks?"

Katie was right. Not long ago, I had worked as a livery stable hand for the same reason, and few people had paid any attention to me.

"You mean, besides us?" I asked. I pointed toward a large outcropping of rocks to our right. "There."

Katie looked at the rocks, then back at me. "I can't see any evidence that someone has been near those rocks recently. Are you sure?"

"Wolf doesn't leave tracks," I said, "but I know my brother."

"I'm sure you know him better than most folks do," she said.

I started to ask her what she meant; but before I had the chance, we found Wolf and Seth. Katie may have been surprised when we rode around the end of the outcropping and found our friends with their guns ready, but I wasn't. They holstered their guns and waited for us to dismount.

Seth laid a folded blanket on a flat rock for Katie; but he, Wolf, and I sat on the bare rocks. Although we rested in the shade, the rocks still held plenty of heat; and the breeze did nothing to cool them—or us.

Wolf and Seth listened as I shared what little information we had gathered. I finished by telling them about our plan to meet at Dan's office that night.

"We'll be there," Wolf said. "We have learned something too." He nodded at Seth.

"We found a new grave half a mile back," Seth said. "It couldn't have been more than a day or two old."

"You think it was a member of this gang we're after?" I asked.

Seth drank from his canteen, then wiped his mouth with his sleeve. "The evidence is strong," he said.

Katie gasped. "You dug up the corpse?" she asked.

"My apologies, Ma'am," Seth said. "We wanted to make certain that the gang had lost a man."

"What did you discover?" I asked. I felt as if I'd been sitting on top of a stove. After laying my Stetson on the rock, I removed my bandana and wiped the sweat from my face and my neck. I spread the bandana beside my hat.

"He'd been shot in the back," Seth said.

'Doesn't make him part of the gang," I said.

"There's more," Seth said. "He was bald."

"Oh," I said, "shot in the back *and* bald—that's different—he was definitely part of the gang!" I looked at Wolf. "Maybe we should be Pinkerton agents instead of bounty hunters,"

Wolf and Seth were both grinning. Wolf spoke first.

"Let him finish," he said. I looked at Seth.

"He was wearing a wig," Seth said, "and a false mustache."

"Shallow grave," Wolf said.

"Buried in a hurry, I reckon," I said.

"That's what we thought too," Seth said.

When I looked at Katie, she was fanning herself with her hat. She looked tired, but she smiled at me.

"If that's everything," I said, "Katie and I will head back to town." I stood, walked to Katie, and held out my hand. "We'll meet at Dan's office as soon as the sun goes down. Come to the back door."

"Huh," Wolf said. "The back door? Because Dan and Burt don't want to be seen talking to an Indian?"

"No," I said. "You know them better than that." I grinned. "I reckon it's because they don't want to be seen talking to a Pinkerton agent."

Chapter 14

⸺•❊•⸺

When Katie and I entered Dan's office just after sundown, Wolf was introducing Seth to the lawmen. After we had poured ourselves coffee, Dan sat at his desk; and the rest of us seated ourselves in a semi-circle, facing him.

Dan and Burt listened as Seth told them about the dead outlaw. Dan looked at Wolf and me.

"You think the other four outlaws are still here in town?" he asked.

"We do," I said. "Have you identified any new folks in town? That grave was less than three days old."

Dan nodded at Burt. "We found nine so far," Burt said. "We don't know exactly when each person came into town, but nobody has been here more than a week." He pulled a folded sheet of paper from one of his vest pockets and a pair of spectacles from another pocket. After putting the spectacles on, he held the paper close to a lamp and ran his calloused finger down the page as he counted the names.

He looked up from the paper. "Two women and seven men," he said.

"You've been a lawman for quite a spell," I said. "Does your gut tell you who we should look at first?"

"There's a gambler I think we should take a look at," he said.

"Did he do something to make you suspicious of him?" I asked.

Dan grinned. "No," he said, "Burt just doesn't like gamblers."

"It ain't just that," Burt said. "This feller plays like he doesn't care whether he wins or loses." He pushed the brim of his hat higher on his forehead. "He acts like he's just playing cards so he has a reason to be here."

I looked at Seth, and he nodded. "I can check him out," he said, "if it's all right with the marshal."

"I'd be obliged," Dan said, "but my friends call me Dan." He looked at Burt. "Anyone else?"

Burt removed his hat and scratched his head. "You'll laugh at me," he said, "but I think something's not right about the new livery hand." He replaced his hat and looked at us. "It's nothing I can put my finger on, but something bothers me about him."

When I looked at Katie, she was smiling at me. She shrugged her shoulders. I smiled as I recalled she had mentioned the livery man earlier.

"I'll talk to him," I said. "Wolf will do more good wandering around and listening to what townsfolk are saying. What about the ladies, Burt?"

"One's old and feeble," Burt said. "She walks with a cane." He stroked his chin. "The other one isn't much more than a girl, but she has a baby. I reckon both ladies are staying in the same boarding house as you and Miss Katie."

"I believe I'm better suited to investigate them than any of you gentlemen are," she said. Nobody disagreed with her.

"Be careful," I said. "Reports say at least one woman rides with the gang. We should assume she's one of these women. She could be dangerous."

"That still leaves five men on Burt's list," I said. I stood, picked up the coffee pot, and poured more coffee for myself and everyone else but Seth, who still had a full cup.

"Three of them are cowboys just passing through," Burt said.

"Maybe they are," Seth said, "and maybe they're not. We still need to watch them, don't we?"

"I'll check out their stories," Burt said, "and see if they're who they say they are."

"That leaves the last two for me," Dan said. "Who are they?"

Burt waved a fly away from his cup and then drank some coffee. "One's a drummer," he said. "He arrived last week in his wagon, and he's been pestering folks by selling his snake oil and other odds and ends." He grinned. "Maybe a bottle or two of his snake oil will help your rheumatism."

"I reckon not," Dan said, "but I'll see if he is who he says he is. Who's the last one on your list?"

Burt took another drink. "He's a schoolteacher."

"Are you pulling my leg?" Dan leaned across his desk with his elbows resting on it.

"No. Sir, I'm not," Burt said. "The man says he's heading for Prescott to begin his new job. You'll recognize him when you see him. He looks like a schoolteacher."

"What do you mean?" Katie asked. She was leaning forward, watching Burt.

"He looked like an eastern dude," Burt said. "You know, one of those little sissy hats—"

"A bowler?" Katie asked.

"Yeah, one of those," Burt said, "and a fancy suit, and spectacles—you know—he looked like a schoolteacher."

Katie's eyes sparkled.

"What are you thinking?" I asked.

She leaned forward. "If we were attending a costume party," she said, "and you all

decided to dress as schoolteachers, how would you dress?"

When I looked at the other men, I was relieved to see that they were as confused as I was. Katie saw our confusion, but she waited for an answer.

"I reckon," I said, "we'd dress like the man Burt just described."

"Yes!" she said. She practically jumped from her chair. "Don't you see? The man Burt described wasn't dressed like a real teacher would dress when he traveled. He was dressed the way a teacher would dress in his schoolhouse—he was wearing a schoolteacher's *costume!* He's one of the gang members!"

"Should we arrest him?" Seth asked.

"Son," Burt said, I can't think of a better way to warn the rest of the gang that we know they're in town."

Seth blushed. "You're right," he said. "We need to follow him to see who's with him, don't we?"

I looked at Dan. "This Pinkerton agent may be young," I said, "but he's a fast learner."

Seth grinned. "If we take turns following him," he said, "he'll be less likely to spot us."

"Allan Pinkerton himself couldn't have come up with a better idea, Seth," Dan said. He finished his coffee, stood, and put on his hat. "Let's call it a night. Tomorrow morning, we can locate our people and start collecting information. If you see the schoolteacher, drop what you're doing and follow him. Unless you learn something that can't wait, we'll meet here again tomorrow night. Be careful; these people are dangerous."

Chapter 15

The next morning, Katie and I had a delicious breakfast at the boarding house. Since both ladies who interested us were also at the table, I finished eating and excused myself. Katie stayed at the table to do some investigating. I left the boarding house an ambled toward the livery.

Wickenburg was awake, but most folks were just beginning their business for the day. When I reached the livery, I was pleased to see my friend and former employer, John Robbins. He was leading a saddled roan mare from the stable. As I crossed the street, he handed the reins to a tall man dressed in a suit and wearing a bowler hat. When he saw the man struggling to mount, John hurried into the livery and returned, carrying a short, low bench. As the man rode away, John watched him, smiling and shaking his head.

"Maybe you should start offering riding lessons, John," I said.

John had already picked up the bench and started into the stable. He stopped and looked over his shoulder at me, grinning.

"Will you need this to mount up for your first lesson?" he asked. He set the bench on the ground, walked toward me, and shook my hand. Still grinning, he put his left hand on my right shoulder. "It's good to see you, Nate. What brings you to Wickenburg—business or pleasure?"

He picked up the bench, and I followed him until he set it against the wall of the first stall. He sat in his chair and waved toward the bench.

"Do you have time to talk?" he asked.

"I do," I said. "In fact, I need your help. I took off my Stetson and set it beside me. "What can you tell me about the new man you hired?"

John removed his hat, leaned his head against the stall, and let out a long breath. "Well," he turned his head toward me. "He's the kind of worker that makes me wish I had you back." He grinned. "I don't reckon you'd consider—"

"I'm obliged for the offer, John," I said, "but I reckon I'll stick to bounty hunting. Do you have a problem with your new man?"

"He's a nice enough young feller," John said. He pulled a red bandana from his pocket, shook it out, and wiped his forehead. "He ain't exactly dumb, but he doesn't know as much about horses and tack as he claims to know." He spread the bandana over the hat in his lap. "Once I show him what to do, he does his work, but it seems to me I'm having to do too much explaining."

"Maybe he just really needed a job," I said.

"Maybe," John said, "but I'd rather train an honest greenhorn than deal with a man who acts like he knows his work when he doesn't." He sighed. "His hands gave him away too."

"What do you mean?" I asked. John's answer confirmed my suspicions.

"Show me your hands—and look at mine," he said. He leaned forward and held out his hand with the palms up. They were tough, calloused hands, and so were mine. "Chet has hands like a banker or a doctor—all soft and smooth—not hands like ours."

John wasn't a hot-tempered man, but I could see he was getting angry. I didn't blame him. "He's better than no help," he said, "but not much. As soon as I can find a real livery man, I'll get rid of him." He stood, put on his hat, and stuffed the bandana back into his pocket. "I'd better get a few stalls cleaned. I wouldn't want Chet to raise blisters on his soft hands."

I stood and put on my Stetson. John grinned, and we shook hands.

"I'd be obliged," I said, "if you could put up with Chet for a few more days even if you find a better helper."

John chuckled and swatted at a horsefly that buzzed around his head. "He has something to do with why you're here, doesn't he?" he asked.

"I reckon he does," I said. I was about to leave when I remembered something else I wanted to ask John. "I know Chet hasn't been here long, but have you noticed if he has any friends in town?"

John crossed his arms and stroked the stubble on his chin. "We don't socialize," he said, "but Chet must be a religious feller." The horsefly was back. John raised his hands slowly, held them still until the fly passed between them, and then clapped them together. Grinning, he opened his hands to dump the dead fly on the ground.

"What makes you think he's religious?" I asked.

"Once I saw him going into the church," he said, "and another time he was talking with the priest."

"Father Barnabas?" I asked. When John raised his eyebrows in surprise, I said, "The cantina was crowded yesterday, so we shared a table while we ate. He seems to be a good man."

"I haven't heard anything bad about him yet," John said. "I hope you'll stop by to visit a few times while you're here."

"I'll be back," I said. I couldn't keep myself from smiling. "I want you to meet someone who came with me. I reckon Wolf and another friend will stop here when they come to town too."

I had reached the doorway and was about to step into the street when John spoke again. "You be careful, Nate," he said.

Looking over my shoulder, I grinned and touched the brim of my Stetson. "Always am," I said.

The boarding house was on the opposite end of town from the livery. I headed in that direction, but I took my time, looking in several of the shops on my side of the street. I wanted to give Katie enough time to investigate the two ladies who interested us. While pretending to look at the goods displayed in the shops, I watched the people inside as well as those on the street.

When I came to a saloon, I decided to get a cup of coffee and see if I was too early for the free lunch. Taking one last look at the other side of the street, I paused and leaned against the building. A man who had to be the schoolteacher was strolling along the boardwalk toward the bank. Seth was about thirty paces behind him, looking at a display in the window of a hatter's shop. The schoolteacher entered the bank; and Seth, after waiting a minute, followed him.

I turned, pushed through the batwing doors, and stepped to one side while my eyes adjusted to the darker interior. About a dozen people were seated at the tables while one man stood at the bar, talking with the barkeep. At first glance, I didn't recognize anyone.

Since there was no food at the end of the bar, I walked to an empty table near a window, laid my hat on the table, and sat. After a few minutes had passed, a tall, stoop-shouldered old man shuffled to my table and set a cup in front of me. When I nodded, he filled the cup with steaming coffee and asked me what I wanted to eat. On his recommendation, I ordered a bowl of stew.

I reckon at some time in my past I'd had coffee as strong as strong as what the old man had brought me, but I couldn't remember when. I blew on it to cool it and then took small sips while I looked around the room. Two tables had single diners like me, and three tables had two people seated at them. The table that caught my attention had four men seated at it, playing poker.

The man facing me looked like a gambler. His clothes, from hat to boots, were clean and looked expensive. He had the hands of a piano player, and his face was expressionless. The men on either side of him were cowboys. Something about the man sitting with his back to me was familiar, but I didn't recognize him until he turned his head to look out the window. The fourth poker player was Burt.

When the stoop-shouldered man brought my stew, I was almost afraid to taste it; but it was delicious. As a rule, I'm not a wasteful person. I ate the stew; but my cup of coffee was still half full when I put on my Stetson, dropped six bits on the table, and walked away.

I left the saloon and walked to the boarding house. The place was so quiet I was almost surprised when Katie answered my knock on her door. The excitement in her eyes told me she had discovered something.

After glancing in both directions, Katie pulled me into her room and closed the door. She threw herself into my arms and kissed me. Not wanting to be rude, I kissed her too. A few minutes later, I had the opportunity to speak.

"Do we need to talk in the parlor instead of here in your room?" I asked. "I don't want my inappropriate behavior to besmirch your good name."

With her arms still around me, Katie looked up and smiled. "I'm more concerned about keeping someone else from hearing what we have to say. We need privacy." She giggled. "I reckon I'll just have to risk having my good name besmirched."

Chapter 16

When Katie insisted I should be the first to share what I'd discovered, I told her about Chet. She listened until I had finished.

"Do you think he's a member of the gang?" she asked.

"I do," I said. "Why are you smiling?"

Katie's eyes were sparkling. "Oh, I just like to hear you say those words, Mr. Landry," she said.

I knew I was blushing. She sat on the edge of her bed while I occupied the room's only chair. When I saw she was starting to get to her feet and head in my direction, I grinned but held out my hand to stop her.

"Wait," I said, "you're supposed to tell me what you discovered about our neighbor ladies."

Katie settled herself back on the edge of the bed. She tried to give me a stern look, but her eyes were sparkling. I couldn't stop myself from smiling.

"Well," I said, "is one of those women part of the gang?" I was hoping for a "yes" or "no" answer, but I had learned from experience that Katie's answers sometimes tended to contain more details than mine did. I reckoned this was going to be one of those times.

"It's not real," Katie said. She was leaning forward, rubbing her hands together. "Don't you want to know how I found out?"

"Yes, Ma'am," I said, "but could we please start with *what* you found out?"

Her brow wrinkled as she tried to understand why I was confused. "The baby isn't real," she said. "It is a rag doll!"

"A rag doll—are you sure?" I asked.

It was Katie's turn to be confused. "I reckon I can tell the difference between a real baby and a rag doll," she said. She smiled. "Their crying is different."

I tried not to laugh. Folding my arms across my chest, I said, "I deserved that. Now that I know what we're talking about, I do want to know how you found out."

Katie couldn't sit still. "Did you notice at breakfast the baby didn't cry?" she asked.

"Well, I reckoned it was—" I said.

"So did I!" she said. "It didn't make any noise at all—no crying, no cooing—nothing!"

"And that's how you knew the baby wasn't real?" I asked. Katie's expression told me I was wrong. She continued to give me her answer.

"I knew I needed to get a look at the baby's face, so guess what I did?"

I guessed. "You poked the baby with your fork?" I asked.

"Really, Nate?" Katie asked. She groaned, fell backwards on the bed, then sat up again. "I 'accidentally' knocked over a cup of steaming coffee," she said, "so it ran in the direction of the younger lady. In her hurry to get out of the way, she exposed the rag doll's face. My suspicions were confirmed."

Katie's eyes sparkled, and she couldn't stop smiling. I was proud of her, but I was troubled too.

"Katie," I said, "do you think she knows you discovered her secret?"

Katie shook her head. "We were too busy cleaning up the mess for her to realize what she'd done," she said.

"So," I said, "counting the dead man Seth and Wolf found, we may have identified three of the gang members."

"I wasn't finished," Katie said. Unable to sit still any longer, she sprang to her feet, stepped directly in front of me and leaned forward until our noses almost touched. "We may have identified *four* of the gang members."

As I watched Katie straighten and begin to pace back and forth in front of me, I wondered if my eyes were sparkling too. I could only think of one explanation.

"Are you saying the older lady belongs to the gang too?" I asked.

"She's not really an older lady," Katie said. "Do you understand what I'm saying?"

I uncrossed my arms and stood. "You mean the older lady was really—"

"Yes!" Katie could barely contain her excitement.

"A rag doll?" I asked.

In one smooth, surprisingly quick movement, she snatched a pillow from the bed and began to thrash me with it. I was laughing too hard to speak; but when I finally got her weapon away from her, I was relieved to see Katie was laughing too.

"She was wearing a wig." Katie said, "and heavy makeup."

I gave her my best skeptical look, and she smiled. She pointed to the chair, and I sat.

"You should have seen how fast she moved," Katie said, "when she thought she was about to get scalded."

I started to speak, but she held a finger to her lips. "They both went to the older lady's room," she said, "and I hid where I could see the door." She smiled. "Half an hour later when I was about to come back here, a saloon girl came out of the room."

"A third woman had been hiding in the room?" I asked.

"Oh, no," Katie smiled and shook her finger at me. "There were only two ladies in the room. One of them changed her clothes."

"So, the older—fake older—woman stayed in her room with the rag doll?" I asked.

Judging by her big grin and her sparkling eyes, I reckoned I was wrong. Katie confirmed my mistake.

"I thought so—at first," she said. "The two women have to be sisters close to the same age. They might even be twins."

"Then what makes you think you weren't looking at the younger woman?" I asked.

Katie was still grinning. She was really enjoying herself. She touched two fingers to the side of her neck.

"In her haste to change," she said, "the lady didn't quite get all of her makeup removed." Katie giggled. "Not bad detective work for a lady who runs a boarding house, eh? I wonder if the Pinkerton Agency could use another female agent."

"I reckon you did some good detecting," I said, "but I don't think you're quite ready for the Pinkertons—or maybe they're not ready for you." I stood and walked to the window. "A real Pinkerton agent would know where she went when she left here." Behind me I heard Katie sigh, and I smiled.

"Maybe she went to a saloon and met with the schoolteacher and the gambler who doesn't seem to care whether or not he wins," Katie said.

When I turned to face her, she was trying not to laugh. She crossed the room and put her arms around me.

"Do you want to talk to Seth about my new job, or shall I?" she asked. She kissed me quickly, and then we were both laughing.

A few minutes later, Katie was sitting on the bed again; and I sat in the chair. Neither of us was laughing.

"If we're right—and I believe we are," I said, "we've identified all the gang members. We still don't know what they're planning to do or when they're planning to do it."

"Whatever they're planning," Katie said, "must involve a large sum of money. Do you know how much is in the bank?"

"No," I said, "but we can ask Dan tonight. If he doesn't know, I reckon he can find out."

"Do we have to wait until tonight to meet with the others?" Katie asked. "Sundown is hours away!"

"We're after some smart folks," I said. "One mistake on our part could scare them away, and then finding them again could be a whole lot of trouble."

Katie sighed. "I know you're right," she said. "I just don't like waiting."

"I don't reckon I know anybody who does," I said, "including me." I stood, took Katie's hand, and pulled her to her feet. "So, Mrs. Whitman, let's walk around town, look in whatever shops you want to investigate, have something to eat when we get hungry, and enjoy each other's company for the rest of the day."

Katie smiled. "Why, Mr. Landry," she said, "it would be my pleasure to accompany you!"

When I told Katie we could look in whatever shops she wanted to investigate, I had no idea she would be curious about so many of them. We used up the better part of two hours getting to the opposite end of town. Although I wasn't interested in most of the items Katie examined, I was interested in her. While she looked at merchandise, I watched the people around us. In my mind, I crossed Chet off my list of gang members. I reckoned he was just a lazy, religious man.

When we reached the last shop on our side, I saw John sitting on a bench inside the livery. I took Katie's hand and led her across the dusty street.

"I want you to meet a friend," I said, "and I want him to meet you."

Inside the livery, we felt some relief from the heat. John had the back doors open, and a breeze improved both the temperature and the smell of the stable. Smiling, he laid his half-eaten sandwich beside him on the bench, snatched off his hat, and stood.

I made the introductions. We talked for a few minutes and then started up the street, leaving John to finish his meal.

"I like him," Katie said. After we had passed the blacksmith's forge, she looked into the window of the first shop.

"John's a good man," I said. "Remind me to tell him he should replace Chet when he gets the chance."

We looked in two of the next three shops and then found ourselves in front of a cantina. Katie smiled at me.

"Something smells good," she said. "Are you hungry?"

"I am," I said. "The food was good last time I ate here."

I followed Katie into the cantina, and we sat at the only empty table. A smiling young woman brought us coffee. When she recommended the beef stew with biscuits, we both ordered it.

Katie and I sat on opposite sides of the table. Our coffee was hot. Holding my cup in both hands, I pretended to blow on it. Katie was watching me.

"See anyone you recognize?" I asked.

She nodded slightly and whispered, "In the corner behind you."

Setting my cup on the table so I could swat at an imaginary fly, I glanced in that direction. I reckon Katie saw my confusion when I looked across the table at her, but she waited for me to speak. After making sure nobody was paying attention to our conversation, I leaned forward and whispered, "How do you know Father Barnabas?"

"Who?" she asked. It was her turn to be confused.

"The priest—Father Barnabas—how do you know him?" I asked. "He's the man at the corner table behind me."

The smiling young lady brought our food, set a bowl in front of each of us, and put a plate full of biscuits between us. We thanked her, and she hurried away.

Katie leaned forward to take a biscuit. "I've never seen him before," she said. "I'm talking about our older friend from the boarding house."

She sat back, dipped the biscuit into her stew, and spoke in a normal tone. "What do you suppose they have in common?" She was smiling as she tasted the biscuit.

"Maybe," I said, "she's confessing her sins."

Since the smiling young lady hadn't brought us butter or jam for our biscuits, I followed Katie's example, took one from the plate, and dipped it in my stew. It was delicious.

We didn't talk much while we ate. I was finishing my second biscuit when the saloon girl walked past our table and out the door. I had eaten a third biscuit and finished my stew when Father Barnabas stopped at our table on his way out of the cantina.

"Good afternoon, Mr. Jackson," he said. "I see God has blessed you with a much better dining companion than you had yesterday."

I introduced Katie and Father Barnabas, and we exchanged pleasantries for a few minutes before he excused himself and left the cantina. Katie and I had another cup of coffee before I paid for our meal and we continued our walk.

Chapter 17

————————•●❀❦●•————————

Katie and I had grown close enough that either of us could tell when something was bothering the other one. By the time we left the second shop, I knew something was troubling her. She had been too quiet.

"You want to head back to the boarding house?" I asked.

She put both hands on my arm and looked up at me. "Would you mind?" she asked.

"Of course not," I said. "Are you feeling ill?"

Katie smiled. "I'm fine," she said.

"Yes, Ma'am," I said, "you certainly are." She squeezed my arm.

We didn't talk much as we walked the rest of the way to the boarding house. When we arrived, the place was quiet; and the parlor was unoccupied. Still holding my arm, Katie led me to a settee. For a while, we sat in silence. I had my arm around her shoulders, and she was snuggled against me.

She moved far enough away from me to see my face. "Do you like Father Barnabas?" she asked.

Her question surprised me. I smiled. "Not as much as I like you," I said.

Katie sighed and leaned farther away from me. "I'm serious," she said. "What's your opinion of him?"

"I don't know him well enough to have much of an opinion," I said. "He was kind and friendly to me, and he seems to treat other folks the same way—no matter who they are. Why do you ask?" Gently I pulled her closer to me.

"I don't know," she said. "It was probably nothing."

This time I pulled away from her so I could see her face. I reckoned "nothing" had to be "something."

"What's troubling you?" I asked. "You may have seen something I missed."

"Don't laugh," Katie said. "Something was wrong with him. It was in his eyes—the way he looked at the saloon girl, and then at me too." Her brow wrinkled as she tried to remember what she was describing. "He wasn't looking at us the way a priest should look at a woman—I'm probably just being silly."

I wasn't laughing. Although I hadn't noticed anything like what Katie had seen, I trusted her intuition the same way I trusted my own "gut" feeling about other things.

She hadn't been looking at me while she was talking. I reached over and gently lifted her chin until her eyes met mine.

"Katie Whitman," I said, "you are an amazing woman. I can think of a lot of words that describe you, but *silly* isn't one of them. We'll keep an eye on Father Barnabas."

Since we had the parlor to ourselves, we stayed there and talked about whatever came to mind—things that had happened in our past lives, things that were happening now, and things we hoped would happen in our future life together.

We had paused in our conversation and were simply enjoying each other's company when Katie squeezed my arm.

"What are you thinking about, Mr. Landry?" she asked.

"Chicken," I said. I leaned back on the settee and looked at the ceiling. "Fried chicken."

"What?" Katie asked. She turned toward me, looking confused.

"I smell fried chicken," I said. "Don't you?"

Katie took a deep breath, then smiled. "I do now!" she said. "We'll have a feast for supper tonight!"

An hour later when I seated Katie at the table, I saw that she'd been right. After we had finished our feast, which ended with dried apple pie, we decided to take another walk. Sundown was close enough that we could end up behind Dan's office just after dark. We timed our stroll perfectly.

Burt grinned when he opened the door in response to my knock. "Come on in, Folks," he said. "I reckon the others will be arriving shortly."

Dan, who was seated at his desk, stood when he saw Katie. He smiled and waved his hand toward the coffee pot.

"Howdy, Folks," he said. "The coffee is fresh. Help yourselves if you've a mind to."

I walked to the stove, picked up the pot after wrapping apiece of leather around its handle, and looked over my shoulder at Katie. She shrugged and smiled.

"Half a cup please," she said.

I carried the cups to where she was seated, handed one to her, and sat beside her just as Wolf and Seth entered the room, followed by Burt. As soon as they had poured their coffee and seated themselves, we got down to business.

When Dan suggested we should hold off drawing conclusions until after everyone had reported his findings, we agreed. He asked Katie to go first.

All of us men listened as she repeated both what she'd told me earlier and what we'd seen at the cantina. Katie and I had decided not to mention her suspicion about Father Barnabas until we learned more about him. When she had finished, Dan nodded at me. I shared what I'd learned about Chet and explained why I didn't think he was part of the gang.

Seth was next. "I think Katie was right about that schoolteacher," he said. "Wolf and I took turns watching him so he wouldn't get suspicious. He sure enough does *look* like a schoolteacher, but he doesn't *act* like one—especially when he doesn't know someone is watching him."

"What do you mean?" Dan asked.

"Well," Seth said, "he seems to have a lot of interest in the bank." He leaned forward in his chair with his hands folded and his forearms resting on his knees. "He doesn't have much interest in children or education."

"Now, how did you come to know that?" Burt asked. "Are you guessing?"

Seth shook his head slowly. "I don't guess," he said. "I observed him and based my conclusions on what I saw and heard." He sipped his coffee. "When I followed him into the bank, I leaned against the wall near the door and watched him. He'd done this before. He asked for the owner—or whoever was in charge. While he was waiting to see the man, he studied everything around him." Seth blew on his coffee to cool it, then took another sip. "He must have deposited a large sum of money because the man showed him the safe to assure him his deposit would be secure. He saw everything he wanted to see."

"You said something about children," Dan said. "How'd you learn about that?"

"Easy," Seth said. He grinned at us and drank a little more coffee. "I followed him to a saloon; we were standing next to each other, and I bought him a beer. We struck up a conversation; and when I mentioned teaching school for a year back in Pennsylvania, he said he reckoned he'd enjoy spending time in a pit full of rattlesnakes more than in a classroom full of whining brats."

"Did you really teach school for a year in Pennsylvania?" Katie asked.

Seth was grinning again. "No, Ma'am," Seth replied. "I've never set foot in Pennsylvania or taught school anywhere, but he didn't know that. I figured if he could pretend to be a schoolteacher, I'd give it a try too. I'm not one to brag, but I think I did a better job than he did."

"Anything else?" I asked.

"I'd finished my beer," Seth said, "and I didn't want to rouse his suspicion; so, I left, and Wolf went in."

"He had another beer," Wolf said, "and ate a free lunch at one of the tables while he talked with a saloon girl."

"Do you know what they talked about?" Dan asked.

"No," Wolf replied. "I asked if I could join them, but they didn't like the idea. I reckon it was because I had never been a schoolteacher."

"Highfalutin snobs," I said. Katie giggled.

"My people are never highfalutin snobs," Wolf said.

Burt chuckled. "I don't reckon they are," he said. "By the way, the cowboys were really cowboys, and they rode out early this morning."

"The drummer left after he'd eaten breakfast," Dan said. Leaning back in his chair, he folded his arms across his chest. "Can any of you think of a reason for not rounding up these four outlaws first thing in the morning?"

No one spoke. When Dan stood, the rest of us did too.

"Let's meet here at sunup," Dan said, "and we'll put an end to this Players Gang. Try to get some rest; I don't reckon this will be an easy job."

Although the sun had set well over an hour earlier, the night was still hot when Katie and I left Dan's office. The breeze that hit us was hot too. We took our time walking back to the boarding house, but I was sweating by the time we stepped into the parlor.

No one else was there, so we sat on the settee where we'd been earlier. I laid my Stetson on the table beside the settee, removed my bandana, and wiped my face. When I started to put my arm around Katie's shoulders, she stopped me.

"Wait," she said. She stood and crossed the room to another table that held a lamp, a pitcher of water, and several glasses. She filled one of the glasses, took a drink, and brought the glass to me. I thanked her, drank a little of the warm water, and set the glass beside my Stetson.

Katie sat down and snuggled against me. She took my left hand in both of hers and gently squeezed it.

"Are you worried about tomorrow?" she asked.

"I'm concerned about keeping you safe," I said. "We've done everything we can to prepare for tomorrow. I reckon we need to trust God to protect us. We have an edge because they don't know we've identified them."

"What about Father Barnabas?" Katie asked.

"Wolf should be able to keep an eye on him," I said. "I'll tell him in the morning about your suspicions."

"Will my suspicions be enough to persuade Wolf to watch Father Barnabas?" she asked.

"Yes, Ma'am," I said.

"How can you know that?" Katie asked. She leaned back far enough to see my face.

"Because," I said, "they're enough to persuade me."

"What can I do to help you tomorrow?" she asked. Katie was still watching me.

"I've been thinking about that," I said. "How do you feel about working with Seth to arrest the women? We have to time this right to make sure nobody can warn the other gang members or escape. If they split up, one of you can follow each of them."

131

Katie turned on the settee and threw her arms around my neck. I couldn't tell if she was laughing or crying, but her body was shaking.

"Thank you, Nate," she said. "I was afraid you were going to tell me to lock myself in my room until you'd captured the gang." She looked up at me again. "I want to help you," she said. "When I can be useful, I want to be a part of what you do. Thank you for allowing me to assist you."

I would have replied to Katie, but I reckoned talking while she was kissing me might be considered rude behavior.

Chapter 18

I had been awake for a while the next morning when someone pounded on my door. As I dressed and walked to the door in the pre-dawn light, I reckoned bad news was waiting for me. I was right. Before he spoke, the look on Burt's face told me something was wrong.

"Those varmints beat us to the draw!" he said. "They robbed the bank during the night and rode out before sunup!"

I closed the door behind me and started to follow Burt.

"Wait for me!" Katie had come out of her room. We waited until she joined us and then started toward the front door again. "What's happened?" she asked.

When Burt repeated what he'd told me, Katie gasped. "Now what will we do?" she asked. "We were going to catch them before they had a chance to steal anything."

"We'll still catch them," I said. "Then we'll make them give back the money they stole."

When we entered the marshal's office—this time through the front door—Dan was standing near his desk, drinking coffee. He waved his hand toward the coffee pot and waited until Burt had closed the door.

"Well, this is a fine kettle of fish!" he said. He rubbed the back of his neck with his left hand. "It's not the meeting we'd intended to have this morning." He sat in his chair and rested his elbows on the desk. "We can discuss our new plan as soon as Seth and Wolf get here. I wonder what's keeping them."

I wondered too. The sun was coming up, and they should have arrived.

"I reckon there's a good reason for their being late," I said.

"Two good reasons," Wolf said.

None of us had heard him when he came in through the back door. All of us sprang from our chairs, and Katie made a sound that was more of a yelp than a scream. Dan, Burt, and I had reached for our guns; but we relaxed when we saw Wolf.

He was grinning as he walked into the office. Following him were the schoolteacher, the gambler, and Seth. Seth was grinning too, but the outlaws looked angry. I reckoned they must not like having their hands tied behind their backs.

"Sorry we're late," Seth said. "We ran into these two as we were riding toward town. They looked tired and hungry, and we heard this place has free room and board."

"We do," Dan said. "Welcome, Gents!"

Burt opened the front door as Wolf waved the outlaws toward it. In a matter of minutes, Burt and I had both outlaws chained to the jail tree. He grinned as we started toward Dan's office.

"Seems like old times, don't it?" he asked.

"It does," I said.

As we walked into Dan's office, Wolf was filling two cups from the coffee pot. He handed one to Seth, and they sat down. Both men looked at the rest of us as they sipped their coffee.

"The gang robbed the bank during the night or early this morning," Dan said. "Good work catching these two."

"They sort of turned themselves in." Seth said. He and Wolf were grinning again. "We asked them if they'd hand over their guns and ride back to town with us, and they did!"

"They might have given up their guns because we were pointing ours at them," Wolf said, "but we can't say for sure."

"Were they carrying any money?" Dan asked.

"Seth and I took ten thousand dollars from them," Wolf said. "We hid it in the desert, and we plan to split it when this is over and we leave Wickenburg."

When Katie giggled, Dan, Burt, Seth, and I smiled. Wolf kept his poker face.

Covering his face with both hands, Dan said, "Sorry. I deserved that. I don't know what I was thinking." He looked at me. "Wolf has spent too much time with you. He's picking up your bad habits."

"Those two," Seth said, "didn't have fifty dollars between them. The two ladies probably took the money and left town headed in the opposite direction."

"Over half the money was gold," Dan said. "Burt and I should be able to catch up with them."

"I'll come with you, if you don't mind," Seth said.

"You're welcome to ride with us—" Dan said. "So are the rest of you." He looked at Wolf, Katie, and me.

"I reckon you three can handle this," I said. "We'll stay here and see if we can learn anything that will help."

"I'll get enough food for all three of us and meet you at the livery," Burt said. He was already moving toward the door.

"We'll fill our canteens—and a couple of extra ones," Dan said. "We'll have the horses saddled by the time you get there."

The lawmen had left; and the three of us stood, facing each other. After a short silence, Katie spoke.

"Why are you looking at me?" she asked.

"You're more pleasant to look at than Wolf is," I said. When I gave her a charming smile, she turned to Wolf.

"Why, Wolf?" she asked. Katie wasn't smiling.

"You are a wise woman," Wolf said, "and we wish you to share your wisdom with us."

"Do you believe the two female outlaws are still in town?" I asked. I could see her relax.

"I do," she said. When I smiled at her, she blushed. "Yes, I believe they're still here." She sat in the closest chair. Wolf and I each moved a chair so we could sit facing her. Her eyes were sparkling as she leaned toward us.

"Put yourselves in their place," she said. "If you needed to escape from the law because you had robbed the bank, and you could either risk your life by riding into the desert or change your appearance and stay in town undetected, which would you choose?"

"Huh," Wolf said. "You and Carmen will become good friends." He looked at me. "She is right, Brother. These cunning women may still be in Wickenburg." Turning back to Katie, he asked, "If you were in their place, how would you escape from town?"

"I would hide the money," she said, "and disguise myself as a person who would draw little or no attention." She leaned back in her chair and folded her hands. "Then I would wait until the search was less intense. Once people had stopped looking so hard, I'd take the money and slip out of town."

"I reckon it's a good thing you're not an outlaw," I said. I stood and offered my hand to Katie. She took it, and I helped her to her feet. As we started toward the door, Wolf rose and followed us.

"So," he said, "if we want to stop the gang from walking away with the money they stole, we need to find these two women, who are hiding behind disguises here in town."

"Yes," I said, "but we also need to find the money if we want these outlaws to go to prison." I looked at Katie.

"Because," she said, "without the money, we can't prove they robbed the bank."

"Huh," Wolf said. "For the same reason, Dan will have to free the two men Seth and I brought in."

I opened the door and held it until Katie and Wolf had stepped outside. Then I followed them and pulled the door closed behind me. We stood, facing the street and watching the folks who walked past us.

"There can't be a hundred people in town," I said, "and fewer than twenty-five of them are women."

"We already know at least a half dozen women we can exclude from our search," Katie said. "We need to be discreet so they don't know we're looking for them. If they get suspicious, they might change their appearance again." Her eyes sparkled as she looked from Wolf to me. "Finding these women may not be as difficult as you think. Gentlemen, let's go hunting!"

As Katie and I walked away from the marshal's office, Wolf said, "Huh!" When I looked over my shoulder, he was heading in the opposite direction, and I knew he was going to hunt in his own way.

We took our time as we wandered toward the other end of town. We checked each shop, watching everyone we met, but pretending to look at no one. Outside the shops, we watched the folks we passed. At the edge of town, we crossed the street and headed in the opposite direction.

By the time we reached the cantina where we had eaten the previous day, Katie and I were both hungry. Only two tables were occupied. I followed Katie to a table beside a window that faced the street. After I had seated her, I took the chair across from her. She smiled and thanked me.

"This way," she said, "we can watch the street while we're eating."

"We can," I said.

A plump, gray-haired woman brought us coffee and recommended tortillas. When Katie agreed to try them, I smiled at the woman and held up two fingers. She turned and shuffled toward the kitchen.

Katie and I sipped our coffee, watched the street, and tried to add more people to our list of folks who we knew weren't disguised outlaws. When the woman returned with our food, we paused in our conversation. We didn't say anything else until she had returned a second time with more coffee. Katie waited until she had left, then leaned toward me.

"You know what we need?" she asked.

I looked around the room, then leaned toward her. "More food?" I asked.

She closed her eyes, took a deep breath, and let it out slowly. I took another bite of my tortilla.

"No," she said. When she opened her eyes, I smiled at her. "We need someone who's lived here for a while— someone who knows everybody."

"You mean," I said, "somebody who could point out two women who are new in town."

Katie's eyes sparkled. "Yes!" she said.

"Do you reckon we could find somebody like that, *and* have more food?" I asked.

Chapter 19

·•➤⋇◄•·

Katie didn't want a second helping, but she waited patiently while I ate. Since she wasn't eating, she continued to talk.

"Dan and Burt are already looking," she said, "but people will be on their guard when lawmen are around. We need someone less threatening."

"I reckon I see the right man for the job," I said, "but you'll have to trust me."

Since Katie sat with her back to the door, she didn't see Father Barnabas when he walked into the cantina. As I motioned for the priest to join us, Katie looked over her shoulder. She groaned softly when she turned back toward me.

"We wanted an opportunity to investigate him," I said. "Looks to me as if God just handed it to us. I'll talk to him so you can watch him."

Father Barnabas smiled as he accepted my invitation to sit with us. "You are most kind, Mr. —"

"Just Nate, remember?" I said. "And this is Katie. I wanted to return the favor of sharing a table, Father Barnabas."

The same woman who had served us brought him coffee and a bowl of stew. Still smiling, he thanked her. After she had left, he noticed we were watching him.

"I order the same thing every day," he said, "so Abigail doesn't even ask me what I want anymore."

He had finished his stew and was wiping the broth from his bowl with a thick slice of bread when Abigail arrived with a second helping of bread, stew, and coffee. She refilled my cup and Katie's too.

Father Barnabas paused to look at us as he was about to take his second bite. He laid his spoon on the plate with his bread and looked from Katie to me.

"You both look troubled," he said. "Is there something I can do to help you?"

"There might be, Father," I said. "Have you been in Wickenburg a long time?"

"Not a long time when compared to eternity," he said, "but I have been here for some time." He was smiling. "Why do you ask?"

While he ate his stew and drank his coffee, I told Father Barnabas what we were trying to discover. By the time I had finished, his bowl was empty. He drank the last of his coffee, set his cup on the table, and leaned back in his chair.

"The information I am about to share with you," he said, "may prove to be of no consequence." He looked at me, at Katie, then back at me. "I make no accusation. I make only an observation. You understand?"

When Katie and I nodded, he started to speak, then stopped. After looking around us to make sure no one was listening, he leaned forward and continued.

"Last week, a helper showed up at the church. She introduced herself as Sister Rebekah. She doesn't know some of the basic things that should have been included in her schooling. At first, I thought she was just dull-witted; but she appears to be quite intelligent in some areas."

"Hold on," I said. "Are you trying to tell us you think this—this *nun* may be part of the gang we're after?"

"Hasn't she been at the church with you the past few days?" Katie asked.

Father Barnabas shrugged his shoulders. "I've seen her once or twice," he said. "I don't really have enough work for her, so she spends most of her time in town, helping others—at least she claims to be helping others."

"Maybe," I said, "she's been helping herself. Do you know where she is now?"

Father Barnabas shook his head. "I can help you find her," he said. Pushing his chair away from the table, he stood. "Remember, I'm not accusing Sister Rebekah of anything. I'm only telling you what I've noticed. If you find her before I do, please tread lightly until you learn the truth."

"Pick one direction on the street," I said. "After I pay for our food, Katie and I will take the other direction."

Katie held on to my arm as we started down the street. Both of us were watching everyone around us.

"Well," I said, "I reckon Father Barnabas should be off your list of suspects now."

"Why would you think that?" Katie asked.

I looked at her. "He is a priest," I said.

"And we're looking for a nun," she said. She looked up at me, smiled, and then turned her attention back to our surroundings.

"The woman *says* she's a nun," I said.

Katie replied without looking at me. "The man *says* he's a priest."

We reached the edge of town without seeing a nun. We were walking in the opposite direction when Katie said, "If this woman is part of the gang and she suspects we're looking for her, she won't still be dressed like a nun."

I had been thinking the same thing. I hoped we were wrong.

"Let's see if Father Barnabas has found her," I said.

"Yes," Katie said, "and let's see if we can find Father Barnabas."

We walked slowly all the way to the church, still watching for Sister Rebekah in case Father Barnabas had missed her. By the time we stepped into the church's dim interior, we had given up hope of finding her.

Then Katie and I saw someone sitting in the front row. We didn't move forward until our eyes had adjusted to the weaker light.

"Too small to be Father Barnabas," I whispered. As we moved closer to the front of the room, I recognized the clothing of a nun.

"Sister Rebekah," Katie said, "may we speak with you?"

When the woman nodded, Katie and I walked to the front bench and seated ourselves on either side of her. She kept her head bowed, blocking our view of her face.

"We're looking for someone," Katie said, "and we thought you might be able to help us."

Sister Rebekah's head remained bowed. At first, I reckoned she wasn't going to answer Katie's question, but then she spoke.

"Having been here for only a little more than a week," she said, "I know few of the town's people. Nevertheless, I shall help you if I can."

"Thank you," Katie said. "You probably heard about the bank robbery. My friend and I are helping the marshal and his—oh—there's a scorpion crawling on you!"

All three of us jumped to our feet. Sister Rebekah said a few words folks wouldn't expect from a nun.

"I'll get it!" Katie said. She grabbed at Sister Rebekah's habit, pulling the head covering loose.

The nun, still between Katie and me, shielded her head with both arms. She couldn't see Katie grinning and holding up the covering like a prize.

"Give me back my bonnet," Sister Rebekah said.

"A real nun," Katie said, "would know it's called a *coif*."

As my surprise at Katie's actions began to wear off, I suspected the reason for what she had done. She confirmed my suspicions when, still smiling, she spoke.

"We need answers now," she said, "and I thought I could save us some time." Katie put her hand under the nun's chin and tilted the woman's head back to reveal her face. "Nate, meet the younger of our two boarding house neighbors." She looked at me with that familiar sparkle in her eyes. "Would you like to ask her some questions?"

"Why don't you question her?" I asked. I couldn't keep the grin from my face. "You two seem to be forming a real friendship."

I reckoned the woman had good control of herself because she didn't hit me. When she looked at me, her eyes told me how much she wanted to.

"Two members of your gang are already chained to the jail tree," Katie said. "We'll take you to see them when we're finished here."

When the woman seated herself again, Katie and I joined her. She sat with her arms folded, staring straight ahead.

"I have two questions," Katie said. "Where's your partner, and where's the money?"

The woman didn't look at Katie. "I have the same answer," she said, "to both questions. Go pound sand."

"I reckon I was wrong," I said, "about that friendship." I stood. "Let's get this naughty nun to the jail tree so we can start hunting the other woman and find the money."

As we walked toward the marshal's office, the woman didn't resist; but she called me some mighty nasty names. I just smiled; and the more I smiled, the angrier she became. By the time we had chained her to the jail tree, that woman was snarling like a cornered mountain lion.

"What did you do to set her off like that?" Burt asked. We had stopped at Dan's office, and Burt had come with us to secure the prisoner. When Katie had discovered the woman was wearing a shirt and britches under her habit, Katie had removed the habit and left it in the marshal's office.

"You can't leave a lady chained to this tree in the company of these—these animals!" she said. "Who are these men, and what have they done?"

"I don't reckon we need to introduce you to these two, Ma'am," I said. "Your play has ended, and your theater is closed. Enjoy visiting with your fellow players."

"You're correct," Katie said. "These men would never chain a lady to this tree; but from where I'm standing, I can't see that they have."

Burt and I looked at each other, but neither of us spoke. When Burt retreated toward the marshal's office, I took Katie's hand gently and led her along as I followed him. Our newest prisoner yelled threats and insults after us.

"Looks like you're right," I said. "We didn't chain a lady to that tree."

Burt paused to let us catch up with him. "Dan and Seth aren't back yet," he said. "I have good news and bad news. Which do you want first?"

"Bad," I said.

"Good," Katie said.

Burt grinned. "Good news it is," he said. "While you two were hunting down the third outlaw, Wolf caught someone he believes is the fourth one."

"What do you mean he *believes* he's caught the fourth one?" I asked.

We had reached the marshal's office. Burt opened the door and stepped aside to allow us to enter. "See for yourself," he said.

Wolf sat on one corner of Dan's desk. The only other person in the room sat in a chair, facing Wolf. As Burt closed the door, the person sprang from his chair and turned to face us. He appeared to be a young man, slightly built, with brown skin and a thin, black mustache. He wore a sombrero and the clothing of a peasant. His eyes widened when he saw us.

"Please help me!" he said. "Save me from this wild savage!"

Wolf crossed his arms over his chest and watched as the man shuffled toward us.

Katie looked at me. "We're hunting for a woman," she said.

I looked past the man at Wolf. He hadn't moved. Dropping his left arm to his side, he raised his right hand to his head; and, using his finger as an imaginary knife, he pretended to scalp himself.

Reaching out without warning, I grabbed the sombrero and pulled it off. I held the hat and the wig attached to it so Katie and Burt could see it. Katie stepped closer to the outlaw and peeled off the fake mustache. The woman's facial features and hair color were a lot like those of the woman we had just chained to the jail tree.

"I reckon," I said, "Wolf was looking for a woman too." I looked at Burt. "Let me guess. The bad news you were about to deliver is this little lady didn't have the money either."

Burt shrugged his shoulders. "Good guess," he said.

Chapter 20

Since we had all four gang members chained to the jail tree, nobody was surprised when Seth and Dan returned to Wickenburg empty-handed. After the two men had washed off the trail dust and eaten a good meal, we met at Dan's office. Burt caught them up on what had happened while they were gone.

"Without the money," Dan said, "we have no proof these folks have broken the law." He ran his fingers through his hair. "Disguising yourself certainly isn't a crime."

Nobody spoke for the next few minutes. We drank our coffee and tried to think of a solution to our problem.

"What about the gang's other robberies?" Burt asked. He slapped his thigh and grinned. "They're wanted in at least a half dozen other places!"

"Nobody knows what they really look like," I said. "They've changed their appearance for each robbery."

"Besides," Dan said, "turning them in for some other robbery won't get our money back. We need to find out where the outlaws hid the money."

"I don't think the two we brought in know where it is," Seth said. He stood, walked to the stove, picked up the coffee pot, and refilled his cup. Looking over his shoulder at the rest of us, he raised the pot. When Burt, Wolf, and I held out our cups, he walked over and filled them before setting the pot back on the stove.

"I agree with Seth," Wolf said, "and I don't think the other one I brought in knows either."

"That only leaves the nun," Katie said. She looked at me. "Do you think she knows where the money is hidden?"

"I don't," I said, "but remember, these folks have earned a living by fooling people—even before they became outlaws."

"How long can you keep your prisoners chained to that tree?" Seth asked. "Finding that money won't be easy. There must be dozens of places they could have hidden it."

"More like hundreds of places," Dan said. "I reckon I can get away with holding them for two days—maybe three."

"Then we'd best get to hunting for that money," Burt said. He finished his coffee and stood.

"I think we should divide the town into sections," Dan said, "and search in pairs. Burt and I will start at the livery and work our way up that side of the street. Wolf and Seth can take the opposite side."

"Katie and I will start at the church" I said, "and work back in this direction until we either find the money or meet Wolf and Seth."

"Maybe they moved the money a little at a time," Katie said, "and Father Barnabas noticed Sister Rebekah making repeated visits to wherever the money is hidden."

"Who is that?" Dan asked.

"Sister Rebekah," Katie said. "Well, she's not really a sister, and her name probably isn't really—"

"No," Dan said, "who is Father Barnabas?"

"You don't know the name of the only priest in Wickenburg?" Katie asked. Her expression showed both surprise and confusion.

Dan looked at Burt, who shrugged his shoulders. "I've seen him around town," Burt said, "but I haven't talked to him. He's only been here about two weeks."

Katie and I looked at each other. "Burt's right," I said. "We'd best start hunting for that money."

I felt a knot in my stomach as we walked toward the church. If what I suspected was true, I had made a mistake that would not only free our prisoners to continue their criminal work but also allow them to escape with the money they had stolen.

Katie and I were both breathing hard by the time we pushed the door to the church open and stepped inside. The room was empty. Katie pointed to a door in the front corner. When I opened it, I found a small room that contained only a table with a lamp on it and a single chair with what looked like a blanket draped over the back of it. When I picked it up, I realized it was the priest's robe. A pair of sandals lay on the floor beneath the chair.

As we left the church and headed up the street, I told Katie what I had found.

"You think Father Barnabas is part of the gang?" she asked.

"He's the leader of the gang," I said. "He has the money, and he's escaping with it."

"How?" Katie asked.

As we approached the livery, we saw John waving goodbye to an old, stoop-shouldered miner, who was headed out of town in a buckboard. When John saw us coming, he smiled and removed his hat.

"Good morning, Nate, Miss Katie," he said. "What brings you here this morning—business or pleasure?"

"Business," I said. "Has anybody left town this morning—particularly anybody in a hurry?"

"Well, let me think," he said. He put his hat on and rubbed his stubbled chin. "A nice young fellow rented the buggy to take his sweetheart for a ride. They should be back in an hour or so if you need to talk to them." He squinted as he tried to remember. "Two gents from out of town left their horses—said they're here on business for a day or two."

John brushed a fly away from his face. "I reckon that's everybody except for old Bill, who just left. He rented the buckboard so he could fetch his equipment from his mining claim." John shook his head slowly. "It's kind of sad. He's giving up and selling his tools for whatever he can get. He says he's just plumb wore out." He looked from Katie to me and smiled. "Can you two sit for a spell? Maybe whoever you're looking for will come along."

We followed John into the stable. Katie and I sat on a bench so we could see the street; and John sat in his chair, facing us.

"I'm caught up on my work," he said, "so I can visit until someone needs help."

I could tell Katie had something on her mind, so I waited for her to open the conversation.

"John," she said, "you said your friend old Bill was headed for his mining claim. Do you know where it is?" John and I smiled. "Did I say something amusing?"

"Well, Miss Katie," John said, "a miner don't usually share the location of his claim with other folks—not even his friends."

Katie blushed. "I'm sorry," she said.

"No reason to be, Ma'am," John said.

"Are you and old Bill good friends?" she asked.

I didn't understand why Katie had asked the question until John answered her.

"I try to be friendly with anyone who stops by here," John said, "but I wouldn't say we were friends. I'd never laid eyes on him until he walked in this morning to rent the buckboard."

When Katie looked at me, I saw the familiar sparkle in her eyes. Gripping the edge of the bench, she leaned forward. "What else do you know about him?" she asked.

"Not much," John said. He rubbed his chin. "He talked a bit while I hitched the horses to the buckboard—nothing important— mostly that staking his claim was a mistake." John sighed. "Poor feller said the gold he found didn't weigh as much as the finger he lost—and it wasn't even his whole finger. I felt plumb bad for the old—"

John stopped when I leapt to my feet. "Which finger?" I asked.

When John didn't answer, I realized I must have startled him. I stepped closer and laid my hand on his shoulder. "Forgive me, my friend," I said, "if I scared you. Which finger was Bill missing?"

"I'm all right," he said. "I reckon from the way you shot off that bench, it must be important. Let me think."

Closing his eyes, John held up two clenched fists level with his shoulders. After a slight hesitation, he extended the little finger on his left hand. He opened his eyes and grinned. "This one," he said.

I shook hands with John. "I'm obliged—we're obliged," I said. I grabbed my saddle and started toward the door. "I reckon the whole town's obliged, John. Would you please saddle Katie's horse for her while I saddle Mac?"

"Where are you headed?" John asked. He carried Katie's saddle and bridle as he followed me into the corral.

I laid the saddle on Mac's back and slipped the bridle over his head. "We're going to find old Bill," I said, "help him load his buckboard, and escort him back to town so he doesn't get lost." I fastened the girth, patted Mac's belly, and made sure the girth was snug before I swung into the saddle.

Katie and I let our horses run for a while. When they slowed to a walk, Katie spoke.

"They almost got away again, didn't they?" she asked.

"Almost," I said.

"If he had worn gloves," she said, "he would have escaped with the money. Dan would have let the other four gang members go for lack of evidence."

"He would," I said.

"They would have continued to rob people," Katie said.

"Until somebody stopped them," I said.

She was quiet for a while. Although we still had at least an hour before noon, the wind was hot against our faces. The only sound I could hear besides the wind was the occasional call of a raven. Then we saw the buzzards. "Do you think he's—"

"No," I said. "He's alive, but I reckon he's reached the place where he hid the money. He's loading it into the buckboard; and when he stops to rest, the buzzards think he might be sick or wounded. They're watching him, hoping he'll be their next meal."

Katie shuddered. "What are we going to do now?" she asked, "capture him?"

"Those rocks off to your right won't give us much shade," I said, "but they're close, and they'll provide a little cover. I don't feel inclined to work up a sweat loading the stolen money into that buckboard." I nudged Mac with my heels; and when he started walking toward the rocks, Katie's horse followed.

We dismounted behind the rocks and drank from our canteens. I poured water into my Stetson and let Mac drink. When I saw Katie's expression, I smiled, poured more water into my hat, and let her horse drink too.

"It's a new hat," she said.

"I know," I said, "and I don't mind sharing mine."

I didn't pay much attention to how long Katie and I spent sitting behind those rocks, but I noticed the day was getting hotter. Each time I wiped the sweat from my face, I spread my bandana on the nearest rock, where it dried quickly. Although I wished I could do the same thing with my shirt, I was thankful to be sitting still instead of loading a buckboard with money from the bank.

When Father Barnabas, old Bill—or whoever the man was—finally climbed onto the buckboard's seat, I couldn't stop myself from grinning. Katie, sitting on the ground with her back against a rock, had dozed off. I laid my hand on her shoulder, and she sat up.

"I'm sorry," she said, "I didn't mean to fall asleep."

"No harm done," I said, "and no point in both of us staying awake." I stood, took Katie's hand, and helped her to her feet. "Our buckboard is loaded; let's go get it."

Chapter 21

————•◦→✤←◦•————

Katie and I watched as the outlaw turned the buckboard away from town. We had mounted our horses, but we hadn't started our chase until we confirmed old Bill's intentions. Waiting for him to come to us would have been much easier—for us and for our horses—than pursuing him across the desert.

"I reckon old Bill just added stealing a buckboard to his list of crimes," I said.

"As much as I hate to mention it," Katie said, "so did your friend, Father Barnabas."

When I looked at Katie, she giggled. "Don't feel bad," she said. "Sometimes women just see things men don't."

"I'll remember that," I said. I couldn't stop myself from grinning.

"I reckon you'd better, Mr. Landry," she said.

We let the horses run long enough to close the gap between us and the buckboard, then slowed them to a trot. Since the outlaw didn't know we were after him, he had no reason to run. I wondered how good this man's acting ability was. When we caught up with him, I discovered it was excellent.

Swinging around the buckboard on the right side, we rode even with the driver's seat. Old Bill looked at us and grinned, showing a mouthful of tobacco-stained teeth.

"Howdy, Folks," he said. "Shore is hot, ain't it?" The old man wore faded brown canvas overalls; a dirty, tan shirt with the sleeves rolled up almost to his elbows; and a tattered black hat with the brim turned up in the front. His face, hands, and forearms looked brown from hours of work in the sun. He looked and sounded nothing like Father Barnabas.

"It is," I said, "and I reckon it's getting hotter with each hour that passes."

He pulled a bandana from his pocket and dabbed the sweat from his face. "What brings you two young'uns out on a day like this?" he asked. "You can't be riding for pleasure."

"You got that right," I said. "We're conducting business."

The old-timer leaned toward us and spit tobacco juice on the ground. Glancing at us, he shook his head.

"Filthy habit," he said.

For half a mile, Katie and I continued to ride along at the slow pace of the buckboard as we talked. As hot as it was, the flies seemed to be chasing us and our horses instead of escaping to some cooler, shady place.

"What kind of business are you folks conducting?" old Bill asked.

I glanced at Katie. The sparkle was back in her eyes. Shifting the reins to my left hand, I slowly drew my six-gun.

"We return things," she said.

The old-timer turned to look at her. "Come again?" he asked.

"We return things," Katie said. "We find things—and people— that are in the wrong place, and we put them where they belong."

Old Bill was shaking his head. "I don't reckon I follow what you're saying, Ma'am," he said.

Katie smiled at him. "Well," Katie said, "if we find a stolen buckboard, for example, we return it to the livery stable."

Old Bill's smile was gone, and he was staring straight ahead. Katie was enjoying herself.

"If we find stolen money," Katie said, "we return it to the bank."

Old Bill pulled the bandana from his pocket and dabbed his face again. Katie wasn't finished yet.

"If we find a missing priest," she said, "disguised as a miner, we haul his carcass back to Wickenburg and chain him to the jail tree with the rest of his gang."

Old Bill had laid his bandana on the seat beside him instead of stuffing it back into his pocket. When he closed the hand that had been resting on it and moved it toward his pocket, I thumbed the hammer back on my six-gun. Raising it to rest on my left arm so the gun was aimed at him, I saw his shoulder muscles tighten.

"You should think hard before you make your next move," I said. "I'd recommend you hand over your weapon. If you haven't killed anybody, you might get out of prison in a few years. Try something stupid, and—well—nobody gets out of Hell."

His shoulders slumped, and he stared at his left hand, which still held the reins. He blew out a long breath between his lips and moved his hand away from the bandana.

"There's a derringer in my pocket," he said, "and a coach gun under the seat."

"Good decision," I said. "Father Barnabas would be proud of you. Now, with your thumb and forefinger, pull that derringer out of your pocket and hand it to me."

After I had tucked the derringer into one of my vest pockets, I held out my hand for the coach gun. I holstered my six-gun, broke open the coach gun, removed the brass cartridges, and tucked them into another pocket. Reaching over with my left hand, I dropped the empty weapon into the bed of the buckboard.

I turned toward Katie and smiled. "Does today seem to you like a good day for returning things?" I asked.

She smiled back at me, her eyes sparkling. "Things and people too," she said. She took a sip from her canteen, replaced the cork, and looped the strap around her saddle horn. "Let's get back to town and find some shade."

Katie and I let our horses walk beside the buckboard, both to save their strength and to avoid the small cloud of dust it raised behind it. The wind had died down, and we couldn't escape the heat.

When we stopped in front of the livery a few hours later, John walked out to greet us with a smile. "No offense," he said, "but you folks look about done in. I thought you two were joshin' me when you said you were riding out to find old Bill in this heat. Do you need some help unloading your tools, Bill? You can store them here for a spell if you've a mind to."

"We're obliged, John," I said, "but you're right about being done in. If you can spare the buckboard for a little longer, we need to find old Bill a place to sit in the shade. We already have a place to store most of what's in the buckboard, and we'll find some volunteers to help us unload. We should be back in less than an hour."

I reckon we took a little more than an hour to return the buckboard, but we left it in John's hands and turned our attention to caring for our horses. We had let them loose in the corral when John came out of the livery, carrying a pick in one hand and a shovel in the other.

"Old Bill left these in the buckboard," he said. "He must've missed 'em when he unloaded."

They were the only tools the outlaw had taken with him. The men who had unloaded the money at the bank had ignored the tools.

"Can you use them?" I asked. "The outfit Bill's going to work for next will supply all the tools he needs."

"I can put them to good use," John said. He was grinning. "They look almost new. If you see old Bill, tell him I'm obliged!"

We had only taken a few steps when John called out. He dragged the pick and the shovel behind him as he caught up with us.

"I forgot to tell you," he said. "An hour or so after you left, Wolf and that young feller stopped by here, looking for you. I told them you went hunting for old Bill."

"What did they say?" I asked.

"Wolf told the young feller not to worry because—" John stopped.

"Because what?" I asked.

He seemed confused. "I don't know that he said why—"

"John," I said, "you can tell us."

He relaxed when he saw both Katie and I were smiling.

"He said you'd be safe with Miss Katie to protect you."

Katie and I were still chuckling when we walked into Dan's office. Since no one else was there, we decided to go back to the boarding house, get cleaned up, and change our clothes.

An hour later, I had bathed, shaved, and put on clean clothes. Knowing Katie would need more time to finish getting ready, I sat in the chair with my feet resting on the windowsill of my room. I had left the door ajar to allow the hot breeze to move the hot air from my room and fill it with more hot air.

I was half asleep when I heard a rifle shot, followed by Katie's scream. Leaping from the chair, I bolted out of my room. Finding Katie's door unlocked, I flung it open. She was lying on the floor near the open window with her back to me. Her shoulder was bleeding.

My heart was hammering as I crossed the room, knelt beside her, and gently rolled her onto her back. A bloody spot on the front of her dress was getting larger.

"No, God," I whispered, "please, don't let me lose her."

When I heard footsteps in the hall, I drew my six-gun and pointed it toward the open door. Seth stopped just inside the door, his eyes wide.

"What happened?" he asked.

"Find a doctor," I said.

I holstered my six-gun and turned back to Katie. I didn't realize I'd been holding my breath until she opened her eyes and I blew it out between my lips. I grabbed a pillow from her bed, lifted her head, and slid the pillow beneath it. Katie winced.

"Somebody shot me!" she said. "Why would anyone want to shoot me?"

"Seth went to fetch a doctor," I said. "Just lie still and don't try to talk." I looked at her wound. "The bullet went straight through — that's good."

"It doesn't feel very good," Katie said.

Seth returned with a skinny little man, who carried a black case.

"This is Doc Sowders," Seth said.

The doctor knelt beside Katie and looked at the wound. "I know you're hurting, Ma'am," he said, "but I reckon I can patch you up good as new." Turning to me, he asked, "Can you two gents move her to the bed? Moving her will cause her some pain, but she'll be more comfortable lying on the bed, and I'll be better able to tend to her wound."

Katie groaned when Seth and I lifted her and laid her on the bed; but as we stepped back to give the doctor room to work, she smiled.

"Thank you," she said.

"No need to hover," the doctor said. "Just move the wash basin over here, and make sure it's full of clean water. After that I'll let you know if I need anything else."

When Seth motioned to me, I followed him into the hall. He pulled the door almost closed behind him before he spoke.

"Wolf and I were on our way here when the shot was fired," he said. "He sent me to check on you and Miss Katie while he went after whoever shot at you." He removed his hat and used his bandana to wipe the sweat from his face. Something was troubling him.

"Keep talking, Pardner," I said.

"Wolf and I reckoned that shot was meant for you," Seth said. "We knew it could have killed you." He swallowed hard. "The look I saw in Wolf's eyes when he lit out after the man who fired that shot will give me nightmares for a long time. You need to stay here with Miss Katie. If I can catch up with Wolf in time, I might be able to stop him from killing that man before we find out why he shot her."

"Be careful," I said. I put my hand on his shoulder. "I'm obliged, Seth."

Chapter 22

———••◆≫◆≪◆••———

W hen Wolf and Seth returned to Wickenburg three days later, Wolf's face revealed no indication of what had happened while they were gone. Seth, however, looked grim; and he said little.

Katie was able to sit up in bed. Doc Sowders reckoned she'd be sitting in a chair within a few days, depending on how much pain she had when she tried to get up. The bullet had missed her bones, and Doc's treatment had prevented infection. She was temporarily staying in an extra room with Doc and his wife.

Wolf, Seth, and I waited until afternoon while Katie was sleeping to meet in Dan's office with him and Burt. Dan sat at his desk. The rest of us sat facing him, drinking coffee and making small talk. Dan set his cup on the desk and looked from Wolf to Seth.

"Well," he said, "which one of you gents wants to tell us what happened when you took off after the skunk who shot Miss Katie?"

When Wolf nodded toward him, Seth leaned forward in his chair, holding his cup in both hands. His expression was grim.

"I caught up with Wolf pretty quickly because I let my horse run," he said. "Wolf was moving carefully in case the assassin turned on him. Once I'd joined him, we proceeded slowly, watching the rocks and brush ahead of us." He sat up, drank some coffee, then leaned forward again. "We trailed the assassin all day without catching sight of him. We stopped at sundown and had a cold camp so we wouldn't get shot in our sleep. We saddled up just before dawn and hit the trail again. I don't think we'd have caught up if the assassin's horse hadn't thrown a shoe and come up lame. We found the shoe lying beside the trail."

"Keep talking," Burt said. He stood, walked to the stove, and picked up the coffee pot. While Burt poured more coffee for the rest of us and refilled his own cup, Seth continued his story.

"We had started up a gradual slope," he said, "when the shooting started. The first bullet creased my horse's flank, but we ducked behind the rocks before the assassin could do any more damage." He took another sip of coffee. "We opened up with our rifles, and pretty soon the return fire stopped."

Seth had been watching us as he talked, but now he stared into his cup. He took a deep breath and let it out slowly. "We worked our way up the slope, one of us moving while the other one covered him, until we found the assassin's body. We—uh—we killed a woman."

Dan and Burt were too stunned to speak; but when I looked at Wolf, he said, "The Dust Devil is gone. She wasn't trying to kill you. She wanted to kill Katie and make you suffer."

"Well, that's good news," Dan said, "and I have more to add to it." He rested his elbows on his desk. "Three deputy marshals should be here the day after tomorrow to escort our prisoners to Yuma. When Burt took food to them the past few days, he heard enough to figure out their plan." He nodded at Burt.

"That bunch is pretty clever," Burt said. "Old Bill—or whatever his name is—was the head of the gang. After the robbery, he slipped out of town somehow and buried the loot. None of the other gang members were worried about being caught because they reckoned without the money, we'd have no way to prove they were guilty of anything. Bill would leave town with the buckboard, pick up the money, and head toward Prescott. The others would catch up with him before he arrived in town. My guess is—" he finished his coffee and wiped his mouth on his sleeve. "They planned to divide the money and drift into town separately to start setting up their next job." He chuckled. "I reckon we closed the final curtain on their performances."

"I'm afraid I also have some bad news," Dan said. "Because nobody knew the identity of these outlaws we've captured—or killed, there may not be any reward money."

I looked at Seth and Wolf, then back at Dan. "Sometimes," I said, "the reward isn't about money. Besides, there's a $1500 reward if anybody they robbed in the past recognizes even one of them."

About an hour later when I went to check on Katie, her door was open; and she was sitting up, reading a book.

"*Pride and Prejudice* or *Jane Eyre?*" I asked.

Smiling, Katie laid the book in her lap. "*The Count of Monte Cristo,*" she replied.

"Ah," I said, "Edmond Dantes is quite a dashing hero!"

Katie shrugged. "I suppose he's all right," she said, "but he can't hold a candle to Nate Landry." She smiled, and I saw the familiar sparkle in her eyes.

"Aww, shucks, Ma'am," I said. "I reckon you've had too much laudanum."

Although our lives were quiet for the most part during the next week, a few significant things happened. The three lawmen collected our prisoners and escorted them out of town, headed for their new home in the recently built Yuma Territorial Prison. The next day Doc Sowders let Katie move back to her room in the boarding house. Two days later Seth informed us that he'd been assigned a new case and was leaving the next morning for Prescott. Since we'd all gotten kind of attached to him, we had supper together at a cantina the night before he left.

As we sat around the table drinking coffee after we had eaten, I noticed something was troubling Seth.

"What's on your mind, Pardner?" I asked.

After staring at his plate in silence for a minute, Seth looked around the table at each of us. He swallowed hard, then took a deep breath.

"I reckon," he said, "you folks are the best friends I've ever had."

"Kid," Burt said, "you must have grown up in a prison."

After we had stopped laughing, Seth continued.

"I just want to make something right before I leave," he said. "I haven't been honest with you about something. It may seem little to you, but it matters to me. I was trained not to use my real name when I'm working on a case." He sipped his coffee, then set his cup on the table. "I didn't know any of you when I started working on this case, so I gave you a false name. My name isn't Seth. It's Ben— Ben Robertson."

"Well, Ben Robertson," I said, "I'm proud to know you." I reached across the table with my right hand. He smiled as he shook it.

"Thank you," he said. After Ben had shaken hands with the other men at the table as well as Katie, Dan spoke.

"You were wrong about something, Ben," he said. "Knowing your real name isn't a small thing—to any of us. Your name matters to us because you matter. I reckon I'm speaking for all of us when I say I hope we can work together again someday."

The final significant thing happened the day before we left Wickenburg. After enjoying a delicious supper, Wolf, Katie, and I sat in the chairs on the boarding house porch, drinking coffee and talking.

"It will be good to return to my home," Katie said. She squeezed my hand. "Will you stay for a while at my house?"

When I hesitated to answer, Wolf surprised me.

"It would be good for you to stay in Phoenix," he said.

"What are you talking about?" I asked.

"When I last saw your cabin," Wolf said, "a woman was living in it."

"Why didn't you tell me sooner?" I asked.

"We had work to do," Wolf said, "and I did not know if you would go back to your cabin."

"Who is this woman?" I asked. "Do I know her?"

"You do not know her," Wolf said. "She is a married woman. Her man left her there to keep her safe while he went away to fight."

"You spoke to her?" I asked. "Did you tell her the cabin belongs to me?"

"I told her you would let her stay in the cabin," Wolf said, "at least until her man returns."

168

I was beginning to get angry as I listened to Wolf's account of how he had practically given my home to a stranger. I was about to speak when Katie squeezed my hand. At the same time, she giggled. I let go of her hand, stood, and turned to face her and Wolf.

"What is wrong with you two?" I asked. I waited until Katie stopped laughing.

"You're an amazing bounty hunter, Nate Landry," she said, "and you do know Wolf better than anyone else does, but watch me and learn. I'm going to ask Wolf two questions. When he answers them, you'll understand." She turned toward Wolf.

"You said Nate doesn't know the woman who is living in his cabin. Do you know her?"

"Yes," Wolf said. Katie grinned.

"What is the lady's name?" she asked.

"Her name is Carmen," Wolf said. "I will return to her tomorrow."

"The cabin is yours, Brother," I said. I sat down. "Yours and Carmen's."

"Thank you," Wolf said. "We have added a new room to the cabin. It is your room."

As long as I own my house," Katie said, "you and Carmen will have a place to stay when you come to Phoenix."

After Katie had collected our empty cups and taken them inside, I handed Wolf a cigar. I bit the tip off the one I still held and spat it into the street. Pulling a lucifer from my pocket, I scratched it on the arm of the chair and lit Wolf's cigar, then mine. We sat without speaking for a few minutes.

"How long have you and Carmen been married?" I asked.

"About a month," Wolf said. He blew out a small cloud of smoke and put the cigar back into his mouth.

"A month!" I said. "Why did you wait so long to tell us?"

Wolf took the cigar from his mouth and examined it. "My people," he said, "do not hurry like white people do."

"No," I said, "I reckon they don't." I sat there for a few minutes, grinning and smoking my cigar. "I'm happy for you and Carmen, Brother."

Wolf looked at me and smiled. "I am happy for you and Katie too, Brother."

I found Katie waiting for me in the parlor. She stood; and, when I was close enough, she put her arms around me and kissed me. We held each other for a few minutes, and then she looked up at me and smiled.

"I don't know about you," she said, "but I'm ready to go home tomorrow."

"I don't reckon I have a home," I said. "Wolf and Carmen own it now. I hope my room at the boarding house is still available."

"I don't know about that," Katie said. "I heard the boarding house is going to have a new owner soon."

"You don't say!" I said. "Anybody I know?"

"I believe the lady's name is—" Katie smiled at me. "Oh, now I remember. Her name is Katie Landry!"

"I'm not worried," I said. "I'll just charm her into giving me free room and board for as long as I want to live there."

Katie giggled. "Good luck with that plan, Mister."

Thank you for reading this book. I hope you found it both interesting and enjoyable. Please take a few minutes to leave a review on Amazon.com, Barnesandnoble.com, Goodreads, BookBub, Facebook, or Instagram.

You can also leave a comment or ask a question at www.marklredmond.com or email me at markredmond53@gmail.com. Photos of you holding a copy of one of my books are always welcome.

Check the next page for a list of all my books. If you visit my website and join my posse, I'll email you updates on new books as they're published; and I'll share news about other things happening in my world. My posse is growing, but there's room for you!

Books by Mark L. Redmond

MIDDLE GRADE SERIES

The Arty Anderson Series

Arty Goes West

Arty and the Hunt for Phantom

Arty and the Texas Ranger

Arty's Long Day

Arty and the Cattle Rustlers

Arty's Tough Trail

The Box M Gang Series

The Box M Gang

The Box M Gang and the Army

BOOKS FOR MORE MATURE READERS

Bounty Hunter Nate Landry Series

Bounty Hunter Nate Landry: Major Issues

Bounty Hunter Nate Landry: Family Fury

Bounty Hunter Nate Landry: Dust Devil

Bounty Hunter Nate Landry: Dangerous Disguises

SHORT STORY COLLECTIONS

Five for the Trail